Nicolas took a p[illegible] 'Do you know th[illegible] [illegible]ared at the face that lo[illegible] back at me. There was something extraordinarily familiar about the girl, though I couldn't for the moment give her a name. She was in her early twenties, with long dark hair, high cheekbones, a wide mouth, a tilted nose that, infuriatingly, suggested a comedienne rather than a serious actress . . .

Of course. The features of the girl in the photograph were almost the same as my own.

I turned quickly to Nicolas. 'Who is she?'

'Her name's Elisabeth. You're not by any means identical – but if you wore your hair in the same way, and her clothes, you could easily pass for her.'

I knew with a sudden sick certainty what was coming next.

'And that's what you're asking me to do?'

Nicolas was watching me steadily, unsmilingly. 'Yes. For a short period – about twenty-four hours – I want you to change places with Elisabeth.'

Also by Hester Rowan in Sphere Books:

OVERTURE IN VENICE

The Linden Tree

HESTER ROWAN

SPHERE BOOKS LIMITED
30/32 Gray's Inn Road, London WC1X 8JL

First published in Great Britain by
William Collins Sons & Co. Ltd. 1977

First Sphere Books edition 1978

TRADE
MARK

Set in Intertype Times

Printed in Great Britain by
Hunt Barnard Printing Ltd.,
Aylesbury, Bucks.

CHAPTER 1

'. . . and so I said to her – Alison? Are you still there?'

I put down my nail file and picked up the receiver again: 'Yes, Mother?'

'Oh good, I was afraid for a minute that we'd been cut off. Well, what I *really* rang to say, dear, is that you will be sure, won't you, to *look after* your Aunt Madge's house while she's away? Yes, I know . . . yes, of course I realise that actresses are just as domesticated as anyone else . . . it's just that Madge is so very pernickety. It's very kind of her to let you use her house, but you know what she's like and I'd hate there to be any unpleasantness when she gets back. So you will be sure to leave everything as you found it, won't you?'

I made noises of hurt dignity and reassurance, but my heart wasn't in them. What's more, my fingers were tightly crossed. Not that there was anything amiss in the house that couldn't be righted by a concentrated session with vacuum cleaner and dusters before my aunt returned; but the shattered gates of the drive were going to be rather more difficult to restore to their original condition.

I couldn't even attempt to disown the damage. It was my appalling misfortune that it coincided, exactly, with a grievous bash in the front off-side wing of Aunt Madge's cherished Renault.

I cleared my throat and changed the subject. 'Yes, of course, don't worry. Has Dad got rid of that bad cold he had when you came up to London to see me?'

'Oh yes, he's quite better now. But if we seemed a

little – well, *lukewarm* about the play, you do understand that it was his cold that put us off? We wouldn't have come when we did, except that you warned us that they were going to take it off so quickly. Such a shame after all those weeks of rehearsal . . . When do you start rehearsing for your next play, dear?'

I crossed my fingers more tightly. 'Oh . . . before very long, I hope. You have to remember that there's a lot of competition, though. It's very difficult.'

'Oh, I'm sure you'll have no trouble! But do ask for a bigger part next time, Alison – and if you could get on television it would be so much more convenient for us. Only you will come home for a few days before you go back to London, won't you? Philip Osborne was asking after you again yesterday – he's doing so well in Customs and Excise and he's really quite good-looking, you know. That terrible acne he had in his teens has hardly left a mark . . . Oh, and did I tell you that they're building some new bungalows just off Cedar Road . . . '

I told myself that it was for the sake of diminishing my father's telephone bill that I invented a caller at the door and rang off; my mother has less idea of the passage of time when she's making a telephone call than she has of the odds against an aspiring actress, and it's no use trying to explain to her about either. But in fact I had slapped down the receiver on the conversation because whenever, not content with finding me a prospective husband, my mother also establishes me in a suburban property equidistant from home and the man's place of work, I am liable to explode with unfilial irritation.

I whirled out of the kitchen door, banged it shut behind me, hastily checked that I hadn't compounded my troubles by breaking the glass, and then walked moodily along the grassy lane that led from the back gate towards the highest cliffs on the north Norfolk coast.

It was an attractive walk, hemmed in on one side by flowering back gardens and on the other by a windswept hawthorn hedge creamy with blossom, but I hardly noticed my surroundings. The telephone conversation had brought my problems jostling round me, and Philip Osborne – with or without the residual craters of acne – was the least of them.

The lane ended at the rear of the mock-Tudor pavilion that faced one of the municipal putting greens and gave a view, sloping down to my left, of the small seaside resort. On my right, another path led back at a sharp angle towards the woods that covered the hills behind the town. Ahead of me and to my immediate right undulated the open turf of the cliff-top, rising to a crest where the cliffs reached their highest point. And beyond the edge of the cliffs stretched the flat blue-grey sea.

I walked towards it, the turf springy under my feet, the salty breeze helping to dissipate my irritation. But the depression remained. Near the edge of the cliff – but not too near because I knew that at that point there was a considerable overhang – I stretched myself on the turf, propped my chin on my hands and contemplated my bleak situation.

Being out of work is no novelty for an actress. 'Resting', we like to call it, but it comes to the same thing; I seemed to have spent most of my career, since leaving Drama School, resting.

Not that I'd been idle. I couldn't afford to be. Between anxious visits to the casting agencies, I spent most of my time in London working – unknown to my parents – in a big store, in order to earn enough to pay the rent of the flat I shared.

When I landed a bit part in a new play, I thought that my luck must have turned. Unfortunately, it had the effect of reducing my income considerably. When the play folded – to no one's surprise except the playwright's – I already owed two weeks' rent. It seemed sensible, then, to leave London and live more cheaply somewhere else while I worked to raise the money I owed.

Going back home to Leicester would, of course, have been cheapest of all, but I wasn't prepared to admit to my parents that my acting career was a flop. So when my aunt mentioned that she was reluctant to put her pet in a cattery while she went abroad for a holiday, my offer to cat-sit was downright enthusiastic.

My devious scheme might have succeeded, too. Although it was early in the season, the hotels were already busy and I found a job that would have enabled me to pay off my debt in full, providing I lived very frugally.

But that was before yesterday, when I had brought my aunt's Renault into contact with her gates . . .

An accident, of course. I was swerving to avoid a stray dog which, having treed her tabby cat, had come rushing guiltily out of the garden when I returned from work. It was true that I shouldn't have encouraged the dog by leaving the gates open; but then, though she'd given me permission, I'd never have borrowed my aunt's car if I hadn't overslept and been so late for work that I was afraid I should lose the job if I wasted a minute.

And now I was in a worse situation than I had been when I arrived in Norfolk. I stared gloomily out at the deceptively blue North Sea, then rolled over on my back, sighed, and lifted my face to the sun. I did a split shift at the hotel, mornings and evenings; I spent every fine afternoon on the cliff-top, and the sun was too precious to waste.

There was no way now that I could extricate myself from my debts. I might just manage to pay the rent I owed, but as for Aunt Madge – who was known to relish a little family unpleasantness now and then – I'd simply have to throw myself on her mercy, give her an indefinite IOU, and promise to cat-sit whenever she needed me for the rest of my life. And then, because I couldn't hope to fool my parents any longer, I'd have to trail back home to Leicester: a prodigal daughter, prepared at last to settle down to a secretarial course and the persistent company of Philip Osborne, whose mother and mine were openly conspiring to see us firmly married and bungalowed . . .

I groaned and sat up, my back to the sea. It was, I had

to admit, a pleasant place to be wretched in. There was no one in sight. I had the cliff-top to myself as I sat despondently on the sun-warmed turf, listening to the rise of the larks and the suck and roar of the waves on the shingle far below.

And then someone appeared.

He came from high up on my left, up and over the crest, running at full pelt as though his life depended on it. On this side of the crest was a steep slope. He slipped, slithered down it in a rush and then paused, balancing himself with one hand on the grass, looking about him as if to get his bearings.

I watched with curiosity. If – for whatever reason – he was looking for cover, he'd find none this side of the woods, a good four hundred yards away; the putting green pavilion on the edge of the town was even further from his present position.

He made up his mind, pushed himself to his feet, and started in the direction of the woods. Then, suddenly, he checked in mid-stride, turned and began to run in my direction, towards the edge of the cliff.

I stared incredulously at the approaching figure. Surely he wasn't hoping to try to climb down the cliff? There was an eighty-foot drop to the rocks and shingle below, a straight drop from the overhang; he'd have no chance at all. I gathered my legs uneasily under me, ready to spring up and warn him.

He neared, his feet thudding heavily on the turf, his stride occasionally faltering as he turned to look over his shoulder. He was somewhere in his late twenties, clean-shaven with dark brown hair, dressed in old jeans and a blue sweater. He looked slim and fit enough, but his movements seemed mechanical and his head rolled as though it was too much of an effort to hold it steady. I could see that he was desperately tired, near the end of his strength. Obviously he had realised that he couldn't make it as far as the wood – but what did he plan to do now?

His face was grim with anxiety, his lips drawn back

with effort. I could hear the harsh intake of his breath. Whoever was behind him must be pushing him very hard. Surely he wasn't . . . ?

Please God he wasn't so desperate that he was going to jump over the cliff!

I leaped up and spread my arms wide, as if to block his path. 'You can't come this way,' I cried. 'There's no path down the cliff, you'll kill yourself! That way, down to the town!'

I pointed urgently towards the pavilion. He glanced, shook his head and suddenly sagged to his knees in front of me.

'I'll never make it,' he gasped, his voice cracking with exhaustion. 'Please, you must help me!'

My instinct was to mutter an excuse, turn and walk firmly away towards the nearest habitation; I've fended for myself in London too long to take appeals for help from strange men at their face value. But this man's exhaustion was perfectly genuine and there was something about his attitude as he knelt, spent, on the turf – the angle of his bowed head, the smooth sunburned skin at the nape of his neck, the heave of his shoulders as he fought for breath, the cleanliness of his thick hair despite the sweat on his face – that made him seem touchingly vulnerable.

I crouched to his level. 'I'm sorry,' I said helplessly, 'but I don't see that there's anything I can do . . . What's the trouble, anyway?'

He looked up at me quickly, wiping the sweat away with the back of his hand. His eyes were brown, green-flecked, fringed with surprisingly long thick lashes that softened the square cut of his face. His chest was still heaving but he had managed to steady his voice.

'Look, I'm sorry to ask you this,' he said. 'I can't explain, there isn't time, but I'm being followed by people who've mistaken me for someone else, and I'm desperate to keep away from them. Oh, it's all a mistake, I've done nothing wrong, I swear. I'll tell you all about it later, but just for now – please?'

He glanced anxiously behind him and then suddenly began to strip off his sweater. I jumped up and backed away, but he gave me an apologetic smile as he emerged from the folds of wool in a white cotton tee-shirt.

'Don't be alarmed, it's just that they're after a man in blue . . . They'll be up and over that hill any minute now – but the point is that they're looking for just one man. They'll take no notice of a couple.'

I remained standing and took one sideways step nearer the town. 'A couple?' I stared at him warily. Was this some extraordinary overture to an assault?

'Oh, please don't misunderstand me! I won't harm you in any way. I won't touch you, I give you my word. But if I can just lie here on the grass near you, they won't realise that I'm the one they were chasing. Will you please let me do that?'

I swallowed hard. It was preposterous, of course. I ought to make a bolt for it now, before he recovered his breath . . .

He was still kneeling, his shoulders tired, his hands resting palm upwards on his thighs in an attitude of exhausted supplication. His long-lashed eyes looked up at me earnestly.

'Please, I beg of you. If – if a cat were being chased by dogs and ran to you, surely you'd give it protection? Can you do less for a fellow human being?'

It was an appeal I couldn't dismiss lightly. Wasn't it only the day before yesterday that – though having once been bitten, I'm wary of dogs – I'd flown out of the house to defend my aunt's tabby against a villainous-looking bull terrier? Could I really do any less for a man if it lay in my power to help him?

'Well . . . I suppose . . . ' I began shakily.

He sighed with relief: 'Thank you.' And then he flopped beside me on the turf, the tell-tale blue sweater rolled underneath him, his back to the crest of the hill. 'Tell me the moment you see them, won't you?'

I nodded and sat down stiffly, a cautious yard away. On the whole, and against all reason, I believed him. But what had led to this extraordinary situation? Why was he being chased? By whom?

And *why* did I believe him? Honestly, now . . . ? Wasn't it simply because he was young and personable, long-limbed and long-lashed – because, in short, I was a gullible woman?

Was he fooling me? Perhaps he was a lone wolf of a holiday-maker who had seen me from a distance and amused himself by planning this novel approach that I'd fallen for so easily. Or possibly – oh no, this didn't bear thinking of – he might even be a psychopath, on the run from his own fantasies; running himself near to exhaustion and then cunningly persuading me to sit beside him until he recovered the strength to attack me . . .

I drew in my breath sharply and inched myself a little further away. Whatever happened, I mustn't panic. I must try to act normally, to give the appearance of co-operation.

His eyes were watching me with steady intensity. 'It's true,' he said, and I was marginally relieved to hear that now he had recovered his breath his voice was perfectly even. 'I'm not imagining things,' he said. 'They'll come. Any minute now . . .'

My mouth was too dry for me to moisten my lips, and my husky voice gave the lie to my words. 'I believed you the first time,' I said.

I sat tight as a high-tension spring, one eye on him, the other watching the crest of the cliff for whoever might be coming: policemen? prison warders? men in white coats?

CHAPTER 2

They appeared almost before I realised it, two men in ordinary casual clothes, drifting up over the top of the hill and standing there, surveying the wide view. One had his hand thrust deep in his bulked-out jacket pocket; the other focused a pair of field-glasses on the edge of the wood.

From the corner of my eye I saw a movement on the grass beside me. He had stretched out his hand, not to touch me but to draw my attention. It was, I thought irrelevantly, a good hand – strong, square, practical, browned and hardened by outdoor activity; trustworthy, I found myself thinking, though where the logic was in my decision I couldn't for the life of me explain.

'Are they there?' he asked quietly.

'Yes – two men. And they've got field-glasses.'

He groaned, turning his face to the grass in despair. 'Oh no! If they've got glasses, this'll never fool them . . . Look, you'd better run while you can – go on, they're dangerous men. You don't want to be involved. Beat it!'

I looked quickly up towards the men on the hill. They were still surveying the wood, pointing to possible paths.

'What about you?' I demanded. 'They haven't looked properly this way yet – why don't you run too?'

He shook his head. 'That'd make it dangerous for you. Anyway, I'm all in. Go on, run while you've got the chance – they won't bother you as long as you're on your own. Run, I tell you!'

Part of me wanted to do just that – had wanted to do it

ever since the man first spoke to me. But if I left him now, I would in effect be betraying the trust he had put in me.

I couldn't do it. I couldn't reassure a frightened animal and then go off and leave it defenceless in full view of its enemies, and I certainly wasn't going to do it to a man. But if I wasn't going to run, I had to protect him to the best of my ability.

As he said, their field-glasses would show them clearly that we were not the friendly couple that they might have assumed at first glance. If I continued to sit several feet from him, stiff with unease, they might well begin to look at him more closely.

Whatever had happened to make them follow him, whatever he'd done or not done, I no longer feared him; I was afraid for him.

The man with the glasses was slowly turning towards us, taking in every detail of the landscape. His companion, the one with his hand in his pocket, was already looking in our direction. He raised his other hand to point, and in a sudden rush of compassion I bent over the man beside me, placed my arm across his shoulders and let my long dark hair fall in a concealing curtain about his head.

*

I stayed still for what seemed like several minutes, terrified that if I looked up it would be to find the men advancing towards us. He was as tense as I was, hardly breathing. My lips were within an inch of his sweat-streaked cheek, my arm was pressed against the shoulder of his damp tee-shirt, but I felt no revulsion, only anxiety. Then, inch by cautious inch, I raised my head sufficiently to peer through the veil of my hair.

Unbelievably, it had worked.

I sat up, smiling with overwhelming relief as I saw the backs of the two men moving at a determined jog towards the woods.

'They've gone!' I breathed.

He raised himself on his elbow and stared after them in awed surprise. 'Incredible . . . ' He sat up and looked at me with a wide, slow smile. 'You were wonderful, you helped me far more than I had any right to hope for. Thank you, I'm more grateful than I can say.'

I felt absurdly pleased with myself. I'd been right, after all, to trust him; and having seen the gorillas who were on his heels, I felt sure I'd been justified in protecting him. The combination of my own smugness and his appreciative smile made me feel positively light-headed, but he jumped to his feet and reminded me of the reality of the situation.

'I must go, while their backs are turned. Can you tell me where the nearest telephone box is? Once I can call some friends I'll be able to get this whole wretched business sorted out.'

There's one down on the promenade, beyond the putting green. But look – ' I was thinking quickly, curious to discover what the chase was all about, anxious to help if I could and – yes, I acknowledged that too – reluctant to see him disappear, ' – look, I'm staying in a house a good deal nearer than that. Why don't you come and telephone from there?'

'May I? I'd be grateful.'

I led the way quickly across the grass in the direction of the lane. We could see the two men far ahead and to our left, about to enter the wood; but as they approached it, they turned to look behind them.

I broke into a run. Probably that was foolish; it would have been more sensible of me to hang back and try to give the appearance that we were simply walking together, but instinctively I began the long run for home. The men watched, one of them lifting his field-glasses, and then they too began to run, cutting diagonally ahead of us across the grass towards the far end of the lane.

I ran faster, alarm pumping adrenalin into my system and giving me a turn of speed I'd never realised I possessed. My companion was beside me as we approached the pavilion, and when I pointed wordlessly towards the lane he caught my hand and took the lead, almost pulling me after him.

Even though there were no people in sight, the sheltered lane spelled safety. Here were gardens and houses, telephones and sanity. I slowed, gasping for breath.

He turned to me urgently. 'One of these houses?'

I nodded, hardly able to formulate the words. '. . . On the next corner . . . white lilac at the gate . . .'

I forced myself to stumble on in his wake, though my side was stitched with cramp and if he hadn't been holding my hand so firmly I'd have doubled up minutes ago. We reached the corner, ducking under the overhanging lilac, and I fumbled for the latch of the back gate, thinking that we were safe.

But at that moment two men pushed their way through the hawthorn hedge just in front of us, hefty men, as gorilla-like as I'd guessed from a distance. They advanced, smiling triumphantly. One of them was holding a hard-edged object in his jacket pocket, and neither of them took his eyes off the man who was with me.

I slipped through the gate and held it open for him 'Run!' I gasped. 'I'll go and ring the police!'

None of them took any notice of me. The man with his hand in his pocket was speaking. 'Very ingenious,' he said. 'You nearly had us fooled, this time. But not quite ingenious enough, I'm afraid.'

My companion laughed.

Not defiantly, nor ironically; but pleasantly, though shortness of breath made it difficult. 'Ah well,' he said, 'I can't expect to win them all.'

'A good try, though,' the gorilla conceded. He drew his hand from his pocket. In it was a heavy metal cigarette case. He flicked it open and offered it. 'Cigarette, sir?'

My companion shook his head, pointing to his chest. 'When I've been running until my lungs ache? What are you trying to do, Carter, kill me?'

And then all three of them burst out laughing.

*

My knees sagged. I leaned on the gate for support, staring incredulously from one to another. The hefty man called Carter turned to me almost immediately, with a smile that relieved the stolidness of his heavy face.

'Sorry, Miss. Do you smoke?'

I stared blankly at the cigarette case and then at the man beside me. 'Do you mind,' I said, trying to make it icy and dignified, but humiliated to hear that I was quavering with lack of breath and fury, 'do you *mind* telling me exactly what's going on?'

Carter coughed over the cigarette he was lighting and said: 'Didn't Mr Allen explain? It's an escape and evasion exercise.'

I began to splutter with indignation and my companion intervened quickly. 'I'm sorry, I'll explain it all in a minute.' He turned to the men. 'Thanks for the run, both of you.'

'Pleasure, sir,' said the broken-nosed man with the field-glasses. 'Always glad of a day out,' he added hopefully, 'any time.'

'Well, we'd better be getting back,' said Carter. 'I'll bring your car around to the front gate, Mr Allen.' He nodded at me approvingly, the broken-nosed man gave me a friendly, crooked smile, and they walked away shoulder to shoulder down the lane.

Allen looked at me apologetically. 'Sorry about all this. Perhaps I could come in and explain . . . ?'

I straightened, closed the gate firmly between us and gave him a more unwelcoming look than I'd ever managed to achieve at Drama School classes; but then this time I meant it.

'I wouldn't dream of letting you set foot in the house,' I said. 'Just because I stupidly believed your story out there on the cliff, and let you make a fool of me, you needn't think I'm going to invite you in! I'm not in the habit of entertaining perfect strangers. I think you'd better go, immediately, before I call the police.'

He smiled. 'Oh, they know me anyway. I'm a local man. And you know me too, or rather you did once. Have you forgotten me completely, Alison?'

CHAPTER 3

I stared at him with uneasy hostility, and then remembered. Of course. The Allen family had a farm only a couple of miles from my aunt's house. When I came to stay during the school holidays, I used to go to the farm to ride one of their ponies. I'd been pony mad at ten and eleven.

But when I was twelve, the pony suddenly lost his place in my affections. I fell in love with Simon Allen. He was training as an RAF pilot: almost twenty, very tall, very dark, head-spinningly handsome. For years, Simon was the focus of my adolescent dreams and I decided, dramatically, that if I couldn't marry him I'd renounce marriage altogether. Even now, although it was years since I'd seen or consciously thought about him, I realised that I subconsciously measured the men I met against his remembered image, and invariably found them wanting.

Memory plays tricks, of course. I had no doubt that Simon now, in the flesh, would prove to be a good deal less god-like than I remembered. But I couldn't believe that he'd shrunk to a moderate six feet, that his hair had become straighter, his eyes lighter, his features more angular; on the other hand, if Simon had been equipped with those lashes, I'd surely have remembered. I could swear that I'd never seen this man before in my life.

And then I recalled something else. Simon had had a younger brother. Thinking hard, I could visualise a long-legged sixteen-year-old who had told silly schoolboy stories, played tiresome practical jokes and openly despised small girls. He had a small scar on his right cheek, caused by a fall from a high beam on to a piece of machinery in one of the farm barns, a scar that would always be visible to anyone who knew where to look.

I peered up at his cheek. 'Oh, it's you, Nicolas,' I said without enthusiasm.

He lifted a finger to the scar. 'You remembered it?'

'Yes – I was there when you did it. You were showing off at the time by trying to run along the beam.'

'That sounds likely,' he admitted. 'And I can remember your lack of sympathy – you took one look at me, shrieked and bolted.'

'Yes, for help.' I suddenly remembered the circumstances of our present meeting, and rounded on him. 'Good grief,' I exploded, 'are you trying to tell me that you knew me as soon as you saw me? And yet you hadn't the decency to say who you were – you went through that wickedly silly game, frightening the life out of me and making me behave like – like – '

I subsided lamely, the memory of the way I had behaved making me hot with humiliation. There was a movement at my feet; the cat Tabitha was purling round my ankles, demanding attention. I bent to pick her up in an attempt to hide my mortified face, but she struggled indignantly to be put down at once. Nicolas Allen gave her a single chirrup, 'Hallo, puss,' and the treacherous little beast lifted herself to the top of the gate in one graceful spring and offered him the privilege of scratching her behind the ears.

He addressed the cat. 'I really do apologise, Alison,' he said. 'I'm afraid that I took advantage of your kindness. If it's any consolation to you, though, Carter and Briggs didn't realise that you didn't know me. They assumed that you'd been waiting there to give me cover.'

It was in fact a considerable consolation, though I had no intention of admitting it. 'I think it was . . . contemptible of you to lie to me as you did,' I said bitterly. 'I never liked you as a boy, and the way we've met today hasn't encouraged me to revise my opinion.'

He gave a wry shrug. 'That's understandable. On the other hand, I've gained nothing but admiration for you. You showed kindness and generosity and courage – there's nothing for you to regret or feel ashamed of about that, is there?'

I refused to be mollified. 'But all for an *exercise* – you frightened me and conned me into helping you just for a stupid game of some kind!'

'Not entirely stupid. I borrowed the idea of escape and evasion exercises from my brother Simon. He's an RAF pilot and they do these exercises as part of their training, to teach them how to evade capture if ever they should have to eject over enemy territory. It's an excellent way of adding interest to cross-country running – it keeps you fit and makes you use your wits at the same time. It's thirsty work though, running four or five miles. You couldn't possibly see your way to letting me have a glass of water, I suppose?'

I hesitated, reluctant to prolong the conversation; and then, for Simon's sake, I opened the gate and said grudgingly, 'You'd better come in.'

Nicolas grinned with relief and ducked his way under the lilac. 'Thank you. I was afraid for a moment that I'd offended you irreparably.'

'Don't think you haven't,' I snapped, marching ahead of him with practised dignity across the shaggy lawn that I'd conveniently forgotten I was supposed to cut. Tabitha led the way in high-tailed hope to the back door, pushed past me into the kitchen when I opened it and positioned herself pointedly by her empty dish.

I handed Nicolas a glass, keeping unwelcomingly straight-faced, but as he moved towards the tap I relented a little.

'There's some orange juice in the fridge,' I said ungraciously, stationing myself at the open door as a hint that he was not expected to prolong his visit.

'Thank you. And you must be thirsty too.' He went to take another glass from the dresser, but I shook my head. In fact I was as thirsty as Aunt Madge's tray of seedlings that I'd only just that morning remembered to water, but I was determined not to make it a social occasion. All I wanted was to get rid of him as quickly as possible – but first I had to know the answer to a question that mystified me.

'But what I don't understand is how on earth you recognised me. It's ten years since we met – you were usually away camping and climbing when I came here in my teens. And yet you knew me when you saw me on the cliff. It's not possible.'

Nicolas had taken the jar of orange juice from the refrigerator and helped himself with appalling generosity. I watched indignantly as my breakfasts for the remainder of the week disappeared down his throat in a long muscular swallow.

He sighed appreciatively and put down his empty glass. 'Delicious, thank you, just what I needed. Oh, I had no trouble in recognising you. You're an actress, after all, and that makes you in a sense public property. I saw you last month in that play at the Court – I'm not surprised that it folded, it really was terrible.'

'Thank you.'

'I didn't say that *you* were terrible. The play didn't give you much scope, though, did it? But you were as convincing as you could be in the circumstances, and at least you looked decorative.'

I gave him a very thin smile. An uncomfortable thought had sowed itself in my mind, taken root and now began to blossom. 'All right, so you'd seen me on stage,' I said slowly. 'You knew me by sight. But surely you'd have been surprised when you found that I was the girl on the cliff . . . unless, of course, you'd been watching me and saw me go there . . . ?'

Nicolas had pulled on his blue sweater and carelessly brushed an untidy wedge of dark hair out of his eyes with his fingers. Now he folded his arms and leaned comfortably against the dresser. 'You're right,' he said calmly. 'I have been keeping an eye on you. You spent every afternoon this week on the cliff, so I knew I had a pretty good chance of finding you there today.'

'You've been – !' He was even more brazen than I'd suspected. 'You have the effrontery to stand there and tell me that you've been spying on me!'

'Oh, not spying,' he reproved. 'Simply taking an understandable interest in an attractive girl who used to be a childhood friend.'

'Rubbish!' I retorted. 'We were never friends and you know it. And if you simply wanted to meet me, why not come backstage at the theatre? Or why not write, care of my aunt? Come off it, Nicolas, you've conned me long enough. What exactly is it that you're after?'

'Strange as it may seem,' he said with a deprecating smile, 'your help. No – ' he lifted his hand as I started to say something indignant, ' – it isn't for myself, so there's no need to tell me what you think of my behaviour. It's a girl of about your own age who needs the help. Look, why don't we sit down while I tell you about it?'

I sat down, rather suddenly, on the bench at the pine table. I was tired, thirsty and thoroughly confused. The cat had been making herself persistently tall and agreeable round Nicolas's legs ever since he opened the refrigerator, and now he took it upon himself to open it again and pour some milk into her dish. She settled to it eagerly, her ringed tail gradually subsiding as she concentrated her energy on the art of lapping.

'Cup of tea?' he offered me hospitably before putting the milk bottle away. I nodded. He filled and switched on the kettle and began to ferret for the teapot, and I was too bemused to offer any guidance.

'When you want to enlist anyone's help, Nicolas,' I said, trying to be patient and reasonable, 'do you usually make a point of approaching them in the way you approached me this afternoon?'

'Very rarely,' he said cheerfully, putting far too much tea in the pot. 'There was a good reason for my behaviour this afternoon, though. I knew what you looked like, you see, and I know your background, but nothing at all about your character. There would be no point in discussing the matter with you if you were a shy or timid girl, and if your reaction to fear was to scream and run. I had to find out what kind of person you are, and the best way to do that seemed to be to put you under some kind of stress. That was why I thought up the escape and evasion exercise and persuaded you that it was for real. I know that it was unfair of me to mislead you and I apologise for it. If you'd panicked, I wouldn't have bothered you any further. As it is, since you acted with courage and presence of mind, I know that you're the ideal person for the job.'

'The job?'

'The job of giving help. Sugar?'

I shook my head impatiently. 'About this girl – ?'

'Ah yes.' He put my cup in front of me and then took a photograph from his wallet. 'Do you know her?' he asked.

I sipped the strong tea as I stared at the face that looked back at me. There was something extraordinarily familiar about the girl, though I couldn't for the moment give her a name. She was in her early twenties, with long dark hair brushed straight back from an oval face, high cheekbones, a wide mouth, a tilted nose that, infuriatingly, suggested a comedienne rather than a serious actress . . .

Of course. As I sat looking at the photograph my free hand was instinctively moving over my face, as though I was looking at myself in a backstage make-up mirror. The features of the girl in the photograph were almost the same as my own.

I turned quickly to Nicolas. 'Who is she?'

'Her name's Elisabeth. You're not by any means identical – there are differences in the shape of the ears and the colour of the eyes, and she's probably an inch or two taller and heavier as well. But superficially there's a strong resemblance. If you wore your hair in the same way, and her clothes, you could easily pass for her.'

I knew with a sudden sick certainty what was coming next, but I had to have it put into words.

'And that's what you're asking me to do?'

Nicolas was watching me steadily, unsmilingly. 'Yes. For a short period – about twenty four hours – I want you to change places with Elisabeth.'

CHAPTER 4

There was a long pause. I pushed my tea aside. Tabitha stretched, yawned and settled in her basket, exhausted after an hour of wakefulness.

Eventually I spoke. 'Why?' I asked bluntly.

'I wish I could tell you the whole story,' Nicolas said, putting down his empty cup, 'but unfortunately I'm not free to do so. It's complicated and confidential. I'll be able to tell you more when you've agreed to help, but briefly the situation is this: Elisabeth has an aged grandmother living some distance from her, who is critically ill. For reasons which you'll understand later, it's very difficult for Elisabeth to visit her grandmother. As things are, she'll only be able to make two separate half-hour visits on successive days at the end of this week. But if you'll agree to change places with her, she can extend her visit for twenty-four hours.'

'You mean . . . you want me to cover her absence? To give her an alibi?'

He shrugged. 'Yes if you want to put it like that. An alibi isn't necessarily criminal, you know?'

It sounded preposterous. 'Oh, for goodness' sake – how could I possibly get away with it? However much we may be alike, everyone who knows her would spot the deception at once.'

'No problem. Her family are all in favour of the arrangement. And as I said, her grandmother lives some distance away, so Elisabeth has to take a few days' holiday to make the visit. She'll be completely unknown, in the city where her grandmother lives, except vaguely by sight to one or two people. That's why it'll be perfectly easy for you to walk out of her grandmother's house pretending to be Elisabeth, while she stays put. After that, you're simply a girl on holiday in a strange city until the following day, when you return to the house and resume your own identity. It won't be difficult at all.'

'But if Elisabeth is on holiday, why can't she visit her grandmother in the normal way? Why go through this performance?'

Nicolas frowned impatiently. 'I told you, there are complications. I can't explain at the moment but you'll understand, I promise you, when the time comes.'

I shook my head. 'No. Sorry, but you'll have to count me out.'

'Why?'

'*Why!* Good grief, Nicolas, you didn't seriously expect me to agree to take part in this mad scheme, did you? It doesn't make sense – it sounds unpleasantly crooked, if you want to know.'

'Crooked?' His eyes widened; he looked genuinely offended. 'It's nothing of the sort, I assure you. I agree that it might sound odd if it came from a stranger, but you know me well enough to know that I'm not dishonest.'

The opening that he offered was too good not to take. I returned his own words, on ice. 'Ah, but I don't, do I? I know what you look like, you see, and I know your family background – but as for your character, I know nothing about that at all. Frankly, all I've learned about you this afternoon is that you make an excellent con-man.'

He glowered. 'It was an act, and I've already explained and apologised for it. If it comes to that, you're an actress too – that's one of the added reasons why you're ideal for changing places with Elisabeth, because you're used to playing a part. But it seems that I misjudged your character. I thought that I'd discovered this afternoon that you're a compassionate person, but now

I find that you're not. You're a professional, obviously. You're not humanitarian enough to use your ability to help another girl, your interest in acting is only for the money.'

I stood up, furious. 'Now wait a minute –'

'No, you wait a minute!' he snapped. 'Here's a girl who urgently needs help, and you are in fact the only person in the world who can give it to her. And here you are with time on your hands, but you're not prepared to give up even twenty-four hours of it so that she can spend a little more time with her dying grandmother . . .'

We had been glaring at each other across the kitchen, but now I wavered under the impact of his scorn. 'That's all very well,' I protested weakly, 'but don't you see how peculiar – how *unlikely* it all sounds?'

He softened fractionally. 'Not to me it doesn't; but then, I know the details. Once you know them, you'll be as anxious to help as I am.'

'How do you come into this?' I asked. 'Is Elisabeth your girl-friend?'

'No, I've never met her. She's the daughter of a man I once met, and he's a friend of friends.'

I turned away and wandered uneasily out into the garden, thinking hard. The afternoon was still beautiful, but I hardly noticed my surroundings. Nicolas's words had stung me; I felt mean, as he intended I should.

I was sorry for Elisabeth, whoever she was . . . But it was no use, I couldn't get involved in her problems, I had problems enough of my own.

Nicolas had followed me out into the sunlight, and I rounded on him.

'It's not as easy for me as you seem to think,' I said bitterly. 'Your crack about acting for money just shows how little you know about the profession. I'm out of work, in debt, and about to be in terrible trouble with my aunt when she gets home. I'm sorry for Elisabeth, but I can't *afford* to go gadding off to help her. If you must know, I'm working as a temporary waitress at the Regent Hotel. I'm due back there at six and I'll be late if I don't start getting ready, so if you'll excuse me –'

He reproved me, but mildly. 'There's no need to sound so defensive about it, Alison. I know what you're doing – I didn't mean to imply that you're being idle. I'm afraid I didn't make it clear that you will, of course, have your expenses paid if you agree to help.'

'I shouldn't get far without,' I commented ungraciously.

'Generous expenses,' he went on, strolling past me to the garage and opening the back door. 'In fact Elisabeth's friends have told me to use my discretion, and I'm sure we can stretch the expenses to cover most of your problems.' He switched on the garage light, edged past the messy paint pots piled on the work-bench and bent to inspect the front off-side wing of my aunt's car. 'Ouch, that's nasty.'

'Don't you dare say anything against women drivers,' I advised him. 'How did you know about it, anyway?'

'Oh, Mrs Thorpe who lives just across the road saw it happen.'

'She would,' I said vindictively.

He straightened and looked at me with reproach, making the most of his ability to reduce me to the size of a worm. 'Mrs Thorpe is a very old lady who is housebound – looking out of the window is one of her few remaining pleasures. My mother knows her, so when I saw the damage to your front gates I called in to see her. You'd provided the big excitement of her week, so she was eager to tell me all about it. She was very complimentary about the way you managed to avoid hitting the dog – I shouldn't be at all surprised if she puts your name forward for some kind of animal lovers' medal.'

'Aunt Madge *would* be pleased,' I said.

Nicolas grinned. 'Yes, well, at least we can avert some of her wrath. As it happens, the local Renault dealer is an uncle of mine; I expect your aunt bought the car from him in the first place. I'm sure I can persuade him to do a rush job and get it fixed before she comes home. And I know a local builder who'll mend the gates too

– we'll get the whole lot done on your expenses. All right?'

'But I haven't agreed to help yet,' I protested, backing into the garden. The prospect of having the worst of my financial problems solved was a temptation difficult to resist, but I refused to be rushed. 'Look, you're sure there's nothing crooked about this business with Elisabeth?'

'It's not even slightly bent, I promise.'

I took a deep breath. 'All right then, I'll think it over tonight and let you know tomorrow.'

He looked at his watch. 'Sorry, Alison. There's a deadline, I'm afraid. You have to decide here and now.'

'But that's impossible!' I protested, instinctively digging in my heels. 'I can't leave just like that! There's my job at the hotel . . . the cat . . . I've got to mow the lawn . . .'

He laughed, turned the key in the lock of the garage door and pocketed it. 'Stop making excuses. I'll give you just ten minutes to pack a bag, enough for three days, and while you're doing it I'll ring the hotel and say you've been suddenly called away – I'm sure they'll survive without your assistance. Then we'll go straight to my home. You'd better stay overnight because we'll have to make a very early start tomorrow. Bring the keys of the Renault and I'll ask my father to organise the work on the car and the gates. Oh, and my young sister Belinda's home from Art School, so she can come over while you're away to feed the cat and mow the lawn. All right *now*?'

The authority in his voice was unmistakable, and I resented it.

'No, it's not all right!' I said indignantly. 'I refuse to be hustled like this. I've got to think it over.'

If I had expected him to become patient and persuasive, I was disappointed. He shrugged. 'That's it, then,' he said curtly. 'I can't waste any more time. If you're not prepared to come now, it's all off.' He looked his contempt and began to walk away.

My troubles, which had been rapidly receding, suddenly turned and came crowding back; I had told Nicolas that I couldn't afford to help Elisabeth, but now I knew I couldn't afford not to.

'Wait,' I called. 'I'll come! Just give me a quarter of an hour – '

He turned back. 'Ten minutes was all I offered,' he said sternly, but the look of relief on his face was so genuine that I made it in twelve.

When we reached the farm, his mother came to the door at the sound of the car. She was still attractive but shorter than I remembered, greying, more comfortably rounded.

'You remember Alison, Mother?'

'Yes, of course. I'm so glad to see you again – it's been a long time.'

'It's lovely to be here again,' I said, glancing at the familiar surroundings. 'But I really am sorry to turn up like this without any warning.'

Mrs Allen looked hospitably puzzled. 'Oh, we knew you were coming, my dear. Nicolas told us that he'd be bringing you to stay the night.'

Her son gave me a bland smile as he carried my bag into the house. There were several things I'd have liked to tell his mother about him, but as none of them were complimentary I kept them to myself.

*

I had assumed, now that I had agreed to help Elisabeth, that Nicolas would tell me the whole story, but there never seemed to be an opportunity. The Allen household was noisily extrovert. Belinda had an Art School friend staying with her, and young local cousins and friends arrived early in the evening to play scratch tennis on the bumpy back lawn.

After he had introduced me, Nicolas disappeared with his father to discuss some new farm buildings. Father and son were distinctly alike: Simon had obviously acquired his dark looks from his mother, but

Nicolas had his father's features and build. There were, though, clear family resemblances between the brothers. Now that he was on home ground, Nicolas reminded me strongly of Simon in a dozen different gestures, tricks of speech . . .

But Nicolas was a different man. Simon, as I remembered him, had had a dash of swank about him; Simon had known he was handsome, had taken it for granted that every girl he met would be weakened by his charm, and had accordingly treated his girl-friends with a patronage that, at the time, I had mistaken for chivalry. At tennis, Simon had always delivered deliberate pat-ball services to girls.

Nicolas though, teased by Belinda's friend into playing tennis with her, offered no concessions. I watched as they played one brief set. He was clearly out of practice and inaccurate, but his powerful service slaughtered her. And afterwards he offered her no apology, but merely smiled and thanked her for the game.

I declined, very firmly, to play tennis with him. Instead, I foolishly allowed his quiet, kindly, pipe-smoking father to introduce me to and annihilate me in a particularly vicious form of croquet.

Supper was a movable feast, a cold buffet eaten either in the farmhouse kitchen or out in the half-tamed garden, and when it was too dark to stay outside we retreated to the dining-room to play Monopoly round the big table. It was all I could do to catch Belinda's attention for a few minutes to ask her to look after my aunt's cat while I was away; but it appeared that she knew all about it already.

Hospitable as the Allens were, their gamesmanship was ruthless. I was saved from an ignominiously early bankruptcy at Monopoly only by Nicolas's announcement that we ought to get some sleep.

'I want to leave here by five-thirty,' he announced. 'I'll lend you an alarm clock, Alison – and mind you're down by five-fifteen, or I'll come and haul you out of bed.'

Belinda looked up from the paper fortune she had amassed at my expense. 'He would, too,' she laughed. 'He's a hard man, my brother. Don't let those long eyelashes of his fool you, Alison – if you're going anywhere with him, he'll expect it to be on his terms.'

'Will he?' I said demurely. I hoped that they would all think that I had good reason to disbelieve her, but already I knew only too well that Belinda was right.

Nicolas patted her dark curly hair as he passed her chair. 'Sweet child. We must remember to bring you a stick of seaside rock.'

Mrs Allen rattled the dice vigorously. For all her placid appearance, she had a shrewd eye for business: having cornered the top slice of the real estate market, she was now intent on putting up enough property to enable her to demand exorbitant rents from hapless callers.

'You won't mind if I don't get up in the morning to see you off, Alison?' she said. 'Now that my husband has sold the dairy herd, it's such a luxury for us to be able to lie in a little. I do think it's sensible of you to make an early start. It's such a long way to Cornwall and the traffic is bound to be bad later. Do have a lovely holiday, both of you.'

I glanced at Nicolas. It was understandable that he had not told his family anything about Elisabeth – after all, he had explained to me that her problems were confidential. In the circumstances, to put out the story that we were going on holiday was reasonable; I wondered only if his choice of location was significant.

He met my eyes and smiled briefly, giving nothing away as he said good-night.

I found it very difficult to go to sleep. I opened the dormer window as wide as possible, catching a drift of perfume from the honeysuckle that grew below, but the chintzy room under the eaves with its sloping floor and sloping walls remained oppressively warm. I lay with only a sheet over me, listening first to the muted sounds from below, then to the family coming up to bed, and finally to the small creaking of the old timbers as the farmhouse settled for the night, worrying over the ordeal that lay ahead.

What stupidity had I let myself in for? Because it was stupid, it must be; I couldn't possibly envisage a situation in which a girl of my age, given a holiday from work and the necessary finance – and the finance must be available, otherwise my expenses couldn't be met so casually – would be unable to visit her grandmother!

And yet . . . whatever else Nicolas might be, he certainly wasn't stupid. There had to be some other, more important reason for the exchange of identity, or Nicolas would not be concerned. So was this exchange merely a cover for something else? What, then? Was there really to be an exchange, or was Nicolas conning me again?

What a fool I'd been, ever to think of letting myself be involved!

Well, there was one very simple way out. I could get up, now, dress, pack, creep downstairs, leave a note for Nicolas to say that I'd changed my mind, and let myself out of the back door. It was only a couple of miles to my aunt's house. I could walk it in no time and be safely back in her spare bed soon after midnight.

There would still be all my old problems, it was true . . . But I could beat them somehow. I'd hitch a lift back home to Leicester, explain about my aunt's car, borrow the money from my father to clear all my debts and then knuckle down to an honest job so that I could repay him. Any plain and straightforward work would be preferable to being caught up any further in this extraordinary situation that Nicolas had tried to talk me into.

I'd be letting Elisabeth down of course . . . but was there really a sick grandmother? Honestly, I'd never heard such an improbable story in my life!

But if it *were* true, and I let her down, Nicolas would despise me.

What of it if he did? Nicolas was nothing to me, it just happened that I liked his family. His brother Simon had been the first love of my life, but I was now an adult – and if Simon meant nothing to me there was no reason why I should care what Nicolas thought about me. If I left the house now, I should probably never see Nicolas again in the whole of my life.

And that, I acknowledged wryly as I checked that the travelling alarm he had lent me was set for five in the morning, was the last thing I wanted to happen.

CHAPTER 5

I crept downstairs next morning with a minute to spare, and found Nicolas in the kitchen brewing one of his pots of paralysingly strong tea. I'm not at my best in the early morning and neither it seemed was he; we avoided each other's eyes, and after a muttered ' 'Morning,' he pushed a cup of tea across the table to me in silence before picking up my bag and taking it out to his car.

It was only as I watched him go that I realised that there was something a little odd about his appearance. His lightweight tweed suit must have been at least five years old. It was well-worn, clean but a little shabby, and the cut was distinctly out of fashion. With it he wore a nondescript shirt and an unremarkable tie. I had realised that Nicolas had none of Simon's dash and glamour, but I hardly expected that he would dress in such an undistinguished, inconspicuous way. I felt obscurely disappointed.

I swallowed some tea, grimaced over it and followed him out to the car. It was broad daylight, a beautiful green and golden summer morning. I settled in the passenger seat and asked: 'Where are we going?'

Nicolas looked at his watch. 'I'll be able to tell you that in about six hours' time.'

I felt fragile and grumpy. 'Oh honestly . . . why not now?'

'You'll know why not as soon as I tell you,' he growled in return. Then as we rolled out of the gate, he added in a more conciliatory tone, 'It's not Cornwall, though.'

It's not easy to sound crushing at five-thirty in the morning, but I had a good try. 'I never thought it would be,' I said.

We went south in silence. When I tried to speak, making some ingenuous remark about the build-up of traffic going with us in the direction of London, he merely switched on the car radio. It was almost eight o'clock, when we were within reach of London's tentacles and I was growing restive with hunger and irritation, when he pulled into the car park of a motel, switched off the engine and gave me a civilised smile.

'Breakfast,' he said, with a simplicity that I could almost find endearing. 'And from now on, of course, you're on expenses, so you've no need to feel indebted.'

I was grateful that he'd made the point; I'd brought with me all the cash I had and it was pathetically little. Enough though, now that we were near London, to make a telephone call. After I'd freshened up I went to the foyer, where Nicolas was waiting for me near the telephone booths.

'You go ahead to the restaurant,' I said. 'I just want to make a telephone call.'

He shook his head. 'Sorry.'

I thought he must have misheard me. 'A telephone call,' I expained. 'Now that we're so near, I want to ring a friend in London – I should just be able to catch him before he goes to work.'

Nicolas raised an enquiring eyebrow. 'Beefy fellow with a moustache like a Corsican bandit?'

'How do you come to know Andrew Brownlow?' I asked in astonishment.

'I don't. But I've been keeping a friendly eye on you, remember.' He looked at me with maddeningly amused disbelief. 'You're surely not serious about him, are you?'

As it happened, I wasn't. But that didn't lessen my annoyance with Nicolas. 'It's absolutely no concern of yours, either way,' I said with brittle dignity. 'But he was going to ring me last night, and I thought I'd let him know that I shall be away for a few days,' I side-stepped to get to one of the telephones, but he moved to block my path.

'Sorry,' he repeated, 'but I'd prefer you not to get in touch with anyone at all until after we get back.'

I stared at him in angry amazement. 'What do you mean?'

'I mean that I don't want you to mention anything about what you're doing to anyone. As I told you, it's confidential.'

'I've no intention of telling him what I'm doing – besides, you're being so cagey that there's nothing for me to tell. This is purely a personal call, and you can't stop me from making it if I want to!'

For a moment, as we faced each other angrily, I thought that he was going to seize my arm and drag me away by force. But then he relaxed, shrugged and turned aside.

'All right. Go ahead, Alison. Make the call if you insist. But the minute you do, the whole deal is off. Go on, ring your hairy friend. And then I'll take you straight to Liverpool Street and put you on a train for Norfolk – and you can pay your own fare.'

I was livid: with Nicolas for his authoritarian behaviour, with myself for the penury that made it impossible for me to rebel. I liked Andrew as a friend, but it didn't matter in the least whether I rang him or not; it was the principle that I minded about. I stalked into the restaurant and in a juvenile gesture of revenge ordered a large and expensive breakfast that I was too choked to eat, feeling angrier than ever when Nicolas calmly and appreciatively disposed of my bacon and eggs as well as his own.

*

After breakfast we drove in silence across London. I watched the signs as we travelled down into Surrey and felt a small surge of satisfaction as I realised that we must be heading for Gatwick.

'I can't possibly go abroad,' I announced, coolly triumphant. 'I haven't brought my passport.'

Nicolas got his own back by driving at least a mile before saying: 'Try the glove compartment.'

I opened it with misgiving. Inside was a brand-new passport, complete with photograph, in the name of Alison Maxwell, height five feet five, hair dark brown, eyes blue.

'Very helpful chap, your theatrical agent,' Nicolas commented. 'Only too anxious to let me have a photograph and a few details. Just sign it, would you, when we stop at the lights?'

Against my will, I felt an undercurrent of excitement. I was born in England but my father had been in the Army and I spent most of the first eight years of my life abroad. I love travel, though during the past four years I'd rarely been able to afford it.

'Why didn't you tell me we were going abroad?' I said, forgetting to be annoyed at his high-handedness. 'There was no need to go to the length of getting a new passport – my own's still valid.'

'I wasn't sure how you'd feel about it.'

'Pleased, of course! I'm not likely to get many chances of free travel.' And then, as I began to realise that being abroad would probably make the exchange with Elisabeth more complicated, caution replaced my eagerness. 'That is, depending on where exactly we're going.'

'Exactly,' he echoed dryly, and refused to say any more.

His timing was effective. Once we reached Gatwick we had to hustle, and there was no opportunity for me to discover our destination. Apparently our flight had been called, and Nicolas hurried me out to the waiting aircraft. Almost as soon as we were aboard, the doors were closed.

It was a medium-sized elderly aircraft, carrying chiefly women and children, and I knew without being told that we were not on a scheduled flight.

'Does this bring back memories for you?' Nicolas asked. 'I expect that you and your mother used to use these Services charter flights when your father was stationed in Germany.'

I could clearly remember several holiday trips back to England from the country that I had grown up to think of as home. 'Is that where we're going, then?' I asked eagerly. 'Germany?'

The cabin warning lights went on and we fastened out seat belts. 'Yes,' he said. The engines began to turn, making the aircraft vibrate. A stewardess finished checking the belts and moved back to her own seat, and the aircraft began its taxi-ing trundle.

'Well, whereabouts in Germany?' I asked, impatient to hear.

'Oh, we'll be landing at one of the RAF bases. Relax, it'll take a few hours to get there.'

I couldn't possibly relax. His unwillingness to tell me more had aroused my suspicion. I realised that Nicolas would not be prepared to discuss Elisabeth's confidential problems in public, but there was something that I urgently needed to know.

Until now, when the aircraft had begun to taxi and it was too late to get off, I had taken it for granted that Elisabeth was English. Nicolas had pronounced the name in the English way. But I knew that, spelled with an 's', it was a German name too. It was true that I had once been able to speak fluent German – but surely he didn't intend . . . he couldn't possibly expect me to impersonate a German girl?

I found it difficult to ask the question. My mouth had suddenly gone dry. 'Is Elisabeth German?'

He didn't answer, making the noise of the engines an excuse for temporary deafness. The aircraft turned on to the runway, paused, and began its take-off run.

As always, the speed and vibration filled me with tension. I hate take-offs and landings, and I refuse to believe anyone who pretends not to. I clutched at the arms of my seat, my innate fear of flying compounded with alarm over the task ahead of me. If Elisabeth was German, it would be trebly difficult for me to impersonate her; not just plain difficult – impossible.

'Look, Nicolas,' I said in his ear, trying not to sound as panicky as I felt, 'I didn't realise what I was letting myself in for. I'm sorry, but if she's not English I can't possibly go through with this scheme of yours.'

He reached out a big warm hand and covered one of mine. Stupidly, humiliatingly, my fingers clung to his as the jets screamed to full power and the aircraft threatened to shake itself to pieces about us. And then, with a sudden miraculous smoothness, we were airborne.

'Yes you can, Alison,' he said gently. 'You're an actress, and you'll rise to the occasion – it'll be the performance of your life, I shouldn't wonder. But now you see why I didn't want to tell you where we were going any sooner. If you'd realised Elisabeth was German, you wouldn't have come, would you?'

Not unless I'd been out of my mind, I thought angrily, trying to pull away. He refused to let go, soothing the back of my hand with his thumb. 'Try to relax,' he said. 'There's no need for you to worry, truly. You won't have to start playing your part until tomorrow, and by then you'll be rested and properly briefed, and you'll have had a chance to practise your German. But remember, Elisabeth isn't known in the place we're going to, so you won't be involved in any long conversations. It'll be easy, I promise you.'

His voice and his touch calmed my fears. Ridiculously – considering that it was solely his doing that I was involved at all – I began to feel grateful to him. I looked at the square sunburned hand holding mine and my spirits lightened at the thought that I might not be required to go through the ordeal of impersonating Elisabeth entirely alone.

'Will you be with me all the time?' I said, trying to make it sound as though I asked merely for information.

'Until the moment when you actually start playing

your part, yes. After that I've a job of my own to do somewhere else, but a friend of Elisabeth's will be there to help you.' He gave me a friendly, appreciative smile. 'I'm only sorry that I shan't be there to see you in action, but I imagine that you'll be glad to see the back of me after I've treated you so badly.'

It was a statement, not a question. He released me without waiting for an answer and my hand felt suddenly cold, small and strangely bereft.

*

The day had clouded, but the aircraft climbed through the grey mist and then levelled in sunlight, travelling east on a carpet of cotton wool. I undid my seat belt and relaxed as far as I was able.

'How do we come to be on this charter flight?' I asked. 'Are you in the Army – or the RAF?'

'Neither. We're on the charter flight simply because it happens to be more convenient. You're here on the strength of being an actress visiting a British base, and I'm here because I'm a civil servant.'

I must have looked incredulous. He laughed. 'It's true – we're not all chairborne, you know.'

For the first time it occurred to me that this might not be simply a private matter. 'This . . . escapade is part of your job, then?'

'Anything to drink, sir?' A tall blonde stewardess was at his elbow with the trolley, and he evaded my question. I took the bitter lemon he bought for me and tried another tactic as soon as she moved on.

'Those men who were with you – the ones who chased you along the cliffs. They called you "sir",' I remembered.

'Oh, we're all in the same department. Very feudal, the Civil Service.'

'Which department?'

'Overseas Trade.'

The answer was too pat. I didn't believe it. Come to that, it was ridiculous that he should expect me to believe it. No one in her senses would seriously imagine that three respectable civil servants from the Department of Overseas Trade would take time off to chase each other along a Norfolk cliff-top, however good a keep-fit exercise it might be.

I sipped my drink, watching him covertly as he smoked one of his occasional cigarettes and drank cold lager. He had a relaxed, almost innocent air about him, but I knew that those unfairly long eyelashes camouflaged a cool determination and a habit of authority.

Remembering my brief, breathless conversation with the men Carter and Briggs, I knew that escape and evasion exercises, such as they thought they were taking part in that day, were not unusual.

And if Nicolas Allen had the status to bring two of his men all the way to Norfolk on such an exercise, for the sole purpose of discovering whether I was sufficiently unflappable to impersonate a German girl, it would be naïve of me to imagine that his work was in any way connected with Overseas Trade.

The obvious alternative, though, was something that I was too scared even to think about.

CHAPTER 6

Nicolas began to ask me about the theatre. It was a transparent conversational device to take my mind off the reason for our journey, but I was grateful for it.

'Was it simply by coincidence that you saw me in the play at the Court?' I asked after I had told him my pathetically brief history as an actress.

'It wasn't coincidence at all. It really was friendly interest – you seem determined not to believe that, but it's true. Your aunt was terribly proud about your being in a London theatre, of course, and told my mother who passed the news on to me. So I had to make a point of going to see you on the stage – I could only remember you as a rather fat little girl in a riding hat and a pair of second-hand jodhpurs, trying to persuade old Benjy, our pony, that he was a show-jumper, and getting dumped on your bottom for your pains. You had guts, though. I always admired the way you climbed back every time he stopped dead at a fence and slid you off.'

'But I still don't see why you didn't come backstage to say hallo, or at least get in touch afterwards.'

'That was what I'd intended to do. At the time, though, we were worrying over Elisabeth's family problem. As it happened, I'd seen her photograph that very day, and the moment you came on stage I saw the resemblance between you. And, of course, I knew that you'd lived in Germany as a child, and spoke German. So I realised at the theatre that you could be the ideal person to help us with our problem, and I knew that it would be best to keep away from you until we'd worked something out.'

I raised an enquiring eyebrow. 'We?'

He gave a bland nod. 'The Department –'

It had been foolish of me to think that I might be able to catch him out. ' – of Overseas Trade,' I chimed in. We both laughed, though I wasn't amused.

'I'm glad that you've taken it so well,' he said.

I glanced meaningly at our fellow passengers. 'Don't think I shan't have some more to say when I get the chance! Oh, I'll go on co-operating. I haven't much option since I seem to be financially dependent on you. Just don't expect me not to make a few objections, that's all.'

We ate – Nicolas ate, I nibbled uneasily at – cold chicken, salad and trifle from plastic trays. As we drank our coffee, Nicolas asked whether my German was rusty.

'Sure to be. It's all of four years since I last had a holiday there.' I recalled something and grinned to myself, hoping that I might have found a perfect let-out. 'It isn't standard German, though, Nicolas. I doubt if I could possibly get away with impersonating Elisabeth – I speak with a regional accent.'

'I know,' he said equably. 'I checked your father's record of Army service. He was a technical man, an electrical engineer, and he did a double tour of duty in Germany on attachment to a small RAF unit based close to the border with East Germany. There were no married quarters available, so he rented a house in the nearest village. You grew up and went to school there, so naturally you picked up the local accent. That was why you were turned down two years ago when you applied to the Ministry of Defence for a job as a linguist.'

I blushed at his infuriating omniscience. It was perfectly true that I'd applied for a linguist's job at the time when I first went to London and realised how short my career as an actress was likely to be. I'd thought that I stood a fair chance of getting the job too, until I heard the examiner's kind, amused comment. The fact that what I actually spoke was Thuringian German had come as an astonishing piece of news, the equivalent of being suddenly told that I spoke broad Dorset English.

'There's nothing wrong with local accents,' I said defensively.

'Nothing at all,' he agreed. 'They're very attractive – heaven forbid that we should all speak a dreary standardised language. And as it happens, your accent is incredibly convenient, because Elisabeth comes from Thuringia and speaks with it too.'

The warning lights went on and the aircraft began to descend. 'Not our stop,' said Nicolas. 'I think that this must be the RAF airfield near Bielefeld where the big Army bases are. Most of the passengers will get off here, but we go a good deal further.'

The descent steepened. 'I always hate take-offs and landings, don't you?' he said kindly, offering me his hand. But much as I wanted to, pride prevented me from taking it.

My foreboding about the exchange with Elisabeth had intensified, overwhelming my fear of flying. My knowledge of the geography of Northern Germany was rusty, but I was fairly sure that if we flew a good deal further east from Bielefeld, the next and only possible stop for a Services charter aircraft would be Berlin.

'Are we going to Tempelhof?' I asked, trying to sound calm.

'No, that's a civil airport. We'll put down at the RAF airfield at Gatow.'

'But that's also in Berlin,' I persisted.

Nicolas smiled at me and commandeered my hand as the aircraft touched down with a bump and a squeal from tortured tyres. 'West Berlin,' he agreed. 'There's a big British Forces community there. It's a fascinating city, you'll love it.'

I refused to be deflected. 'And that's where Elisabeth's grandmother lives – in West Berlin?'

'Yes.'

My mind was racing inexorably to a conclusion that I would very much prefer to avoid. 'So Elisabeth has to travel to Berlin to visit her grandmother? And where is she staying now, West – or East Berlin?'

The shake of his head was almost imperceptible, but he gave my fingers a painful, warning squeeze. I snatched my hand away and sat apprehensively while tired children stumbled out of the aircraft with their mothers to finish the journey to Army married quarters by road.

I hardly needed to be told any more. I could work it out for myself.

As a child, I had lived in a village on the extreme western fringe of the Thuringian forest. Thuringia proper was in East Germany. If Elisabeth came from Thuringia, she was almost certainly an East German – and that meant that the only part of Berlin she could be staying in now was East Berlin.

And now it was all clear to me, clearer and even more frightening that I'd suspected when I first boarded the aircraft and found that Elisabeth spoke German.

Elisabeth couldn't visit her grandmother in the normal way because free movement between East and West Germany and East and West Berlin is forbidden by the East German government. Presumably she had been able to obtain permission for two very brief visits; she could make a longer stay in West Berlin only if someone went to East Berlin to cover her absence.

Someone who looked like her.

Me.

Nicolas had promised that what he was asking me to do was not dishonest, and in moral terms he was right. Of course there was nothing *dishonest* about Elisabeth's intention to go from East to West Berlin to spend twenty-four hours with her sick grandmother, nothing crooked, nothing even slightly bent.

It was, quite simply, in East German terms, strictly illegal.

CHAPTER 7

I didn't even notice the take-off. I sat with my arms folded, as though by hugging myself I could keep the flutters of panic in my chest from rising to my throat. I was wretchedly conscious that Nicolas was watching me, dispassionately assessing my reactions.

This, I knew instinctively, was the point of no return. I'd already told him that I would co-operate, but that was before I realised the danger inherent in what he wanted me to do. Now that I'd guessed what was involved, I had the right to think again and make up my mind once and for all.

There was, after all, no way in which he could force me to change places with Elisabeth. It was entirely up to me to decide. Even my lack of money for the return fare no longer mattered – I could ask for help from the RAF authorities at the airfield where we landed. If I said No now, that would be the end of it.

There would be no need even to argue with Nicolas. All I had to do was to let my self-control go, to let fear take over and the tears flow, and he would, I knew, release me from our bargain. Not out of kindness or consideration for me, but simply because a girl who cried would be unreliable, a danger to Elisabeth and others as well as to herself.

I glanced at him as he sat coolly waiting for me to make up my mind and I knew immediately that his good opinion mattered to me too much to allow me to back out. If I failed him now, that would be the end of our relationship.

What I needed was courage. I very much wanted him to take my hand again, so that I could feel the warmth and strength and reassurance of his touch, but I was glad that he didn't because I would only clutch at him, revealing my fears. I looked down, letting my hands fall on my lap and clenching them together, welcoming the pain as my nails dug into my palms, trying to give myself the courage that I didn't naturally possess.

My hair had swung forward across my face. Nicolas bent his head towards me so that he could speak softly without fear of being overheard, and his breath stirred my hair. He lifted a strand of it and smoothed it gently back behind my ear as he whispered: 'There's nothing to worry about, Alison, truly. Do you think I'd let you do it if it were likely to be dangerous? It's absurdly simple – you'll realise that, just as soon as I can get a chance to tell you the details.'

I managed a wan smile. I couldn't trust myself to speak.

'It's still a lot to ask of you, I know that,' he went on, 'but look at it this way. By now, Elisabeth will have a message that everything is arranged and she'll be relying on you to do your part. It's nerve-racking for her, too, you know, and she's in a much worse position than you are. After all, it's not in the least illegal for you to visit East Berlin – they welcome tourists. She's the one who's at risk, not you.'

That wasn't entirely true, and I knew it. Once she was in West Berlin, Elisabeth would be in no danger at all. But although the East Germans might welcome tourists, I wasn't going in as a tourist. I was going in for the purpose of helping Elisabeth to evade the East German laws, and that would make me, as long as I was on their territory, a criminal. There were a good many Westerners in East German jails to prove the point. I was sure that I had read newspaper reports of an English girl currently serving a five-year sentence for helping her East German boy-friend in an attempt to escape to the West.

My face felt cold as the blood suddenly drained from it at the thought. 'Elisabeth's not – ' I whispered back ' – she's not trying to *escape*, is she?'

The lines at the outer corners of his eyes creased with silent laughter. He slipped one hand comfortingly under my arm and gave me a reassuring squeeze. 'Of course not, silly! She doesn't want to, she's happy enough where she is. Besides, if she did, that'd leave you stuck over there! You don't imagine I'd do that to you, do you?'

I had to admit that it seemed unlikely, but there was another point that I wanted cleared up before I committed myself.

'There's something else behind this, though, isn't there, Nicolas?' I whispered. 'I mean, you're not doing all this just to help her spend a little longer with her grandmother?'

He hesitated a moment before replying: 'Yes, of course there's something else. I didn't expect you to believe that there isn't.'

'So this is just a cover?'

He shrugged, but his eyes held a look of warning. Obviously he was not prepared to discuss it with me. Certainly not here, and probably not ever.

I drew a deep breath. 'All right, I won't pester you with questions. But I have to know this: do you promise me that what you've told me so far is true? That Elisabeth really is going to visit her grandmother? Because if this is just something that you've made up to get me here, another confidence trick like the one you played me on the cliffs, I'll – I simply can't go through with it!'

Nicolas stretched out his hand, placed one finger on my chin and turned my face towards him. His own was serious, his green-flecked eyes behind the maddeningly long lashes unsmiling. Absurdly, irrelevantly, I noticed that he needed a shave.

'What I've told you about Elisabeth is absolutely true,' he said quietly, taking away his hand. 'Her grandmother brought her up in Thuringia, because her mother died when Elisabeth was still a baby. Most of their relatives lived in West Berlin, and as soon as the old lady reached pensionable age she came to the West to join them. As you probably know, the East German government insists on keeping its working-age population inside its own frontiers, or the economy of the country would collapse – but there's no objection if old people want to leave. But now the old lady is dying and Elisabeth is virtually alone because her father is in a psychiatric hospital. So you can see how desperately anxious she is to spend as long as she can with her grandmother. Just spare her one day out of your life, Alison, and then we'll have you safely back home, I promise.'

We looked at each other seriously for a few moments and then he smiled, first with his eyes and then with his lips; and I knew that I was irrevocably committed.

*

The approach to the airfield was extraordinarily rural. Nicolas had told me that Gatow was on the extreme western fringe of West Berlin, but I had hardly expected that our descent would be made over a wide flat landscape of forests and lakes, the largest of which lay betweeen the airfield and the city.

We were taken to a transit hotel provided at the base for civilian visitors. Nicolas gave me an hour to rest, shower and change, and then he collected me in a hired dark blue Volkswagen Beetle. Within a few minutes of leaving the gates of the airfield we were driving along a quiet residential road. On one side were dignified late Victorian stucco-fronted villas, set in gardens brilliant with rhododendrons and azaleas, and on the other were the spreading waters of the Havel, Berlin's largest lake, as wide as Windermere.

When I was a child and we lived in our quiet German village, I had often heard my father mention the plight of the city of West Berlin. It was, he said, a political island, a piece of West German territory set, by accident of war, in the middle of Communist East Germany.

I had felt sorry for the West Berliners. I loved the open air, and because I imagined that any city must be entirely built up, it seemed to me cruelly wrong that the inhabitants of West Berlin should be kept cooped up among bricks and mortar, unable to obtain free access to the surrounding countryside.

Now I realised that, deplorable as their political isolation might be, the West Berliners had no need to go short of fresh air. It was late afternoon but the sun was still hot and the Havel was busy with sailing boats, their brilliant spinnakers hoisted to catch every puff of the light breeze.

Presently we drove through woodland and came to the sandy shore of a bay. It formed an ideal lakeside family resort, with a restaurant, open-air cafés, paddling and boating pools for children. The beach was littered with sunbathers, and beyond them the rippling green waves bobbed with the disembodied heads of swimmers.

Nicolas pulled into a car park, grinning at my surprise.

'Not quite what you'd expect to find in Berlin, is it? What I'd really like to do now, of course, is to relax – but unfortunately we're here on business. We need to talk in private, and it's a pity to waste the sun by sitting in the car, so let's take a boat out.'

We skirted the bathing beach and approached a jetty. 'Can you handle a sailing boat?' he asked, his face lighting with pleasure at the sight of some of the dinghies rocking at their moorings.

I shook my head regretfully. 'My uncle was going to teach me. He kept a dinghy at Blakeney, but Aunt Madge sold it after he died.'

'I know – as a matter of fact, she sold it to my father. I got the boat as a twenty-first birthday present, and I've had years of pleasure out of her. I never seem to get much chance to sail now, though. Would you . . . ?'

He sobered suddenly. 'No, we'd better not waste time.

I want to go out on the lake because it's the most private place to talk, but it'll be more sensible to take one of the power boats.'

He hired one and we zoomed away from the jetty and the resort, skimming the glistening waves as we dodged the other boats on the lake. It was fun, a brief open-air holiday, and the speed and the spray and the sunshine helped me to relax. Nicolas still wore his nondescript suit, but he had taken off his jacket and tie. He had changed his shirt, I noticed, for one that looked from the cut of its collar and sleeves as though it had been bought in Germany.

He steered towards a small wooded island, closing the throttle as we approached, so that we drifted in quietly. There were notices proclaiming that it was a bird sanctuary and forbidding landing. Nicolas cut the engine and tied up to a convenient willow branch that leaned across the dark green water, and then stretched out his long legs as comfortably as possible in the cramped cockpit.

We said nothing for several minutes. The sounds of the lake were all about us, the soft splash of diving birds and leaping fish, the ripple and slap of the waves on the hull of the boat, the song of the birds from their island sanctuary. The boat rocked gently and the wispy fronds of willow teased the sunlight, making dancing patterns on our faces, our hands, our bodies.

Our closeness seemed suddenly intolerable. I was aware of him with every nerve, aware of his wind-roughened hair, the sound of his breathing, the shape of his face, the fact that he had shaved, the fact that his hand on the seat was no more than two inches away from mine.

It seemed difficult for me to breathe at all, impossible to move a muscle without making contact with him and betraying the other fact, that I wanted to touch him. Slowly, very slowly, I raised my eyes to look at his face. Our eyes met, in momentary acknowledgement that the attraction was mutual.

And then a background hum grew to a steady roar and rose to a screaming crescendo as a passenger jet flew low overhead, and the tension was broken. We both stirred, laughed a little self-consciously and rearranged ourselves.

'I was going to describe the place as idyllic,' he said, 'but unfortunately we seem to be right under the Templehof flight-path.'

'It's a beautiful lake, though,' I agreed, as the noise of the jet died away. 'I was going to say, "Lucky West Berliners", but then I remembered the Wall. How far are we from that?'

Nicolas pointed away to the east, where I could see nothing but trees.

'The Wall separating West from East Berlin is – oh – say about ten miles in that direction,' he said. 'It's a big city. But we're right on the edge of West Berlin here, and only about five hundred yards from the East German border. Look.'

He was pointing towards the south-western end of the lake where it began to narrow sharply. The sun was coming from that direction and it was difficult to see clearly, but there appeared to be a glittering line stretching from shore to shore just above water level.

'Wire,' Nicolas said succinctly. 'There isn't just the dividing Wall across the centre of the city – the East Germans have put a hundred-mile wire and concrete girdle round the whole of West Berlin, to stop the people on their side from getting in. That end of the lake is in East German territory, and there's a net of steel mesh in the water to stop either boats or swimmers from coming through. They've got high-speed armed patrol boats on their part of the lake too, to stop anyone from coming near enough to make a break for it.'

I shivered and he gave my hand a brief friendly pat. 'Oh, don't worry. You're going through one of the legitimate crossing points in the Wall, and you'll be chauffeur-driven and escorted there and back by a trusted East German government official – wrongly trusted by them, as it happens, but thoroughly trusted by us. Now listen carefully and I'll tell you the plan. We'd better speak in German, though, from now on, just to get you in practice.'

I sat looking out across the water as he talked, so that I could concentrate on what he was telling me without being disturbed and distracted by his presence. His German was infinitely better than mine, fluent and idiomatic but elegant as well. He had, I remembered hearing from my aunt, read modern languages at university. At first, when I asked questions, I was almost ashamed to demonstrate my own earthy Thuringian, but he gave no sign of noticing its oddities and I gradually felt my childhood fluency and confidence returning.

'Why is the East German government prepared to let Elisabeth across the border at all?' I asked when he'd told me the plan in detail. 'I didn't think they allowed any visits to the West.'

'They didn't, until a year or two ago. Now they've agreed to a treaty which allows Westerners to visit the East, and also allows East Germans to make compassionate visits to close West German relatives. I doubt if it was easy for Elisabeth to get permission even so, but Kurt Braun, the official who's escorting her, has obviously pulled a lot of strings. I understand that she's a good East German citizen, so they've no reason to mistrust her.'

'But if she's a good East German citizen, why is she prepared to deceive them by letting me take her place? Why is one day here so much more important for her than two short visits?'

Nicolas smiled distantly. 'There are good reasons.'

'Which you're not prepared to tell me?'

'Which I have no intention of telling you. In our department, we work on what we call a "need to know" basis. What you don't know, you can't talk about.'

'You mean – if I'm caught?'

He put a hand on my shoulder and gave me a sharp,

affectionate shake. 'You won't *be* caught, Alison. Especially not with Braun looking after you. And now that you know the plan, you must admit that your job's not in the least difficult.'

It wasn't difficult, that was true. Nicolas wasn't, as I'd feared, asking me to *do* anything in East Berlin – simply to be there. It sounded extraordinarily simple, almost fireproof.

'Do you know this man Braun well?' I asked.

'We've never actually met, as it happens. But we've worked in co-operation for several years and I feel as though I know him very well indeed. Obviously I can't say whether you'll like him, but I do know that you can trust him. Look, you're getting chilly out here. Let's go and find some coffee.'

He started the engine, turned out into the lake without making too much noise and disturbing the birds, and then opened the throttle and headed back for the shore, slapping breezily over the waves. A passenger steamer cruised past us, the occupants waving and laughing as we bounced across their wake, and I waved back. I was certainly happier about the exchange, now that I knew exactly what was going to happen; if only Nicolas had been going to stay with me all the time, I felt that I could almost enjoy the adventure.

'What will you be doing while I'm out on my job?' I asked in English as he joined me after paying for the boat and we walked towards one of the café gardens.

He shrugged noncommittally. 'Oh, a little business of my own.'

We sat under the shade of a blue and orange umbrella and I watched him as he ordered coffee and two slices of strawberry torte piled with fresh cream.

He caught my eye. 'I made a point of shaving before coming out, so I imagine that it's my suit you're looking at with such disapproval?'

'I did wonder about it,' I agreed.

'Then don't,' he said sharply. 'Don't wonder about things, Alison. Don't ask questions, don't search for reasons, don't concern yourself about anything except what you're actually doing. In this job, it isn't healthy.'

A momentary chill of fear made me catch my breath, but I tried to laugh.

'You and the Department of Overseas Trade!' I scoffed.

But I had no appetite at all for strawberry torte.

CHAPTER 8

After we'd drunk our coffee, Nicolas took me on a sight-seeing tour of West Berlin. He drove back through the woods, through a village with its old church and inn, and along a main road between small weekend bungalows set in well-tended gardens. And then we reached a busy suburb and turned east along a wide straight artery that led to the heart of the city.

As he drove, between buildings that were rarely more than a quarter of a century old, Nicolas pointed out the sights: the Olympic stadium, the steep grassy hills that were actually mounds of wartime rubble, and the flowery acres of the Tiergarten park. At the far end of the road, straddling it, rose the massive arch of the Brandenburg Gate, topped by a glittering newly gilded statue of a chariot drawn by four stallions.

'The road on the other side of the Gate is the Unter den Linden,' Nicolas told me. 'Apparently it used to be the great main street of pre-war Berlin, leading straight up to the royal palace.'

'A lovely name to give to the main street of a capital city,' I mused. ' "Under the linden trees" . . . linden's a much nicer name for them than our lime, isn't it? Are the linden trees still there?'

'New ones, since the war – though the street's now rather dull and lined with government buildings instead of big stores and theatres and hotels. The Gate and the Unter den Linden are both in East Berlin now, of course.'

As he spoke he followed the stream of traffic, turning sharply right instead of driving straight up to the

Brandenburg Gate. I looked back in the direction we had been heading, and saw why. The splendid avenue, leading through the Tiergarten and on through the Gate to become the Unter den Linden, was permanently blocked by a great grey concrete barrier topped by barbed wire. We had reached the frontier and had been turned aside by the Wall dividing West from East Berlin.

'The Wall's quite a tourist attraction, I believe,' Nicolas was saying casually as he drove into the busy centre of West Berlin. 'There are viewing platforms on this side so that people can climb up and look over at the East, if they've nothing better to do. We have, I'm glad to say – we're out to enjoy ourselves for the evening.'

It was tactful of him, I thought. I'd seen newspaper photographs and television documentaries, and I knew that East Berlin was unlikely to be a comforting sight. I didn't want to look at the armed guards who patrolled on the other side of the Wall, the death strip that had been cleared of houses to give the guards a clear field of fire against any would-be escaper, the wreaths and crosses that the West Berliners had hung on their side of the Wall as pathetic memorials to those East Germans who had tried to defy the guards and hadn't made it.

We parked and then strolled along the glittering main street, the Kurfürstendamm. Nicolas was indulgent, encouraging me to window-shop for elegantly-designed porcelain, silverware and clothes; but finally he complained of thirst, steered me to a pavement table outside one of the restaurants, and ordered a bottle of white wine.

'This is Mosel,' he announced as he poured me a glass. 'It's German wine pressed from grapes grown in the German valley of the river, and I do object to the English practice of calling it Moselle, as though it were a French wine. Well . . . ' he lifted his glass and touched it lightly against mine, ' . . . to you, Alison – with many thanks and a great deal of admiration.'

I was too uncertain of myself to want to meet his eyes. The attraction between us was undeniable; we had mutually, mutely acknowledged our admiration. But what he was talking about now was something different, and I knew that he had it all wrong. I wasn't in the least courageous, it was nothing but folly that kept me there beside him, because if I had any real courage I would get up and walk straight out of his dangerous life.

There were, after all, other men. I'd known physical attraction before. 'Surely to goodness, Alison Maxwell,' I scolded myself silently, 'you're not so desperate for a man that you have to get involved with one who probably – almost certainly – works for British Intelligence? He's simply using you. Get up and go girl, before you're in any deeper.'

But foolishly, wretchedly, I stayed. My smile in answer to his toast must have been wan, but he didn't appear to notice it. He had become quiet, preoccupied, frowning as he absently fingered the dark green baroque stem of his wine glass.

Suddenly he said: 'Do you know what I sometimes long to do Alison? I'd love to tell the Department to find someone else to do their dirty work! I'm sick of being given lofty orders that I have to carry out whether I agree with them or not. I'm sick of being pushed about, and having to push other people about in my turn. I've got to the stage where I've a good mind to tell them to keep their job!'

His outburst came as a complete surprise. I'd begun to think of him as a dedicated agent of the government, ruthlessly – as they do in television spy series – making use of any girl who happened to be at hand. This put him in an agreeably new light. I drank some wine and looked at him with renewed interest.

'I'd assumed that you were a career man – that you were devoted to the Department of Overseas Trade.'

He gave me a sombre smile of acknowledgement. 'That's what I thought, until recently. I joined because it sounded really interesting: a chance to use my languages, plenty of travel, a certain amount of excitement. Actually a lot of it is tedious, and some of it downright sordid, but it offers a good career as long as you remember to keep a low profile in situations where you're likely to be used for target practice. But spending this last week at home on the farm has made me realise that I want more out of life than I can ever get from this job. I'm seriously thinking of chucking in the civil service and going into partnership with my father on the farm.'

'Putting down roots?' I asked, carefully keeping my voice light and the question casual as I drained my glass of wine. The Mosel was delicious: cool, delicate, flowery, but with a hint of slate that kept its fragrance dry.

'Yes, that's it – putting down roots, in every sense. I want stability for myself and the chance to produce something useful for the community. I'm tired of rushing about. I want to *belong* somewhere.'

Our eyes met across the table and we smiled understandingly at each other. I felt buoyant, as though I were suddenly floating six feet above the crowded Ku'damm. Nicolas refilled my glass and then said: 'Look, shall we eat here? It's a pleasant evening and a shame to go indoors. I hope you're hungry because I am, and the food they brought to the next table smells delicious.'

'Have you discussed the farming idea with your father?' I asked when he had ordered, taking another heady gulp of wine.

'Only indirectly, so far. He'd always hoped that my brother would join him – Simon was the practical one, I was always labelled as academic. But now Simon's all set for a fullscale RAF career, and he's turned down my father's offer – which incidentally, included an empty farmhouse. Dad dropped a few heavy hints when he told me that Simon wasn't interested, and I'm sure he'd renew the offer if I ask. The problem is, though, that it's no life for a single man. I'm too used to independence to go back to living at home, but on the other hand I really can't face the prospect of rattling about on my own in a five-bedroomed farmhouse.'

I concentrated on my glass, smoothing away with my fingers the last misty traces of condensation left on the bowl by the coolness of the wine. 'That's understandable,' I heard myself saying, and I admired myself for the detachment that my voice achieved.

'It's a beautiful house, though,' Nicolas said eagerly, propping his elbows on the table as he leaned across to communicate his enthusiasm to me. 'I had a good look at it one day during the week, while you were working at the hotel. Mind you, it's been empty for a couple of years and it needs to be renovated and modernised, but it'll make a magnificent home. It's late Georgian and I particularly admire that period – do you?'

I nodded. I do like Georgian architecture, but if he'd said Ming Dynasty I'd probably have nodded just the same; I was light-headed with vintage Mosel and anticipatory happiness.

'The façade's something like this,' he went on, taking a pen from his pocket and making a rapid sketch on the back of the menu of an elegantly-proportioned house, with two windows on either side of the pedimented front door, balanced by five windows on the second storey. 'There are some rather squalid Victorian outbuildings tacked on to the back at the moment, but I'd knock them down and build a new kitchen wing.'

I murmured gravely that a new kitchen wing sounded admirable.

'There's a walled garden, though it's more like a walled nettle bed at the moment,' he explained. 'Oh, and an avenue of lime trees leading up from the road. They could do with a bit of surgery, and there ought to be some selective felling and re-planting, but it's a magnificent feature.'

'Linden trees,' I reproved him gently, 'not lime.'

He laughed and sat back. 'You're right, linden. Ah, this looks like our meal. And mind you eat it, Alison, you've hardly had any food today.'

The agreeable nip of appetite reminded me that this was true. Nicolas seemed to have an unfortunate penchant for making me either angry or frightened just as were were about to eat, and putting me off. But now, as I eyed the crisp roast goose, the green salad, the golden-brown puff-balls of potato, I felt that I could do them justice – if only to please him.

It was happening too quickly, of course. Common sense told me sternly that no real or permanent attachment could come about at this speed. But then, whoever suggested that emotion owes anything to common sense? I knew what I felt for Nicolas was more than merely physical, that for the first time in my life – excepting, that is, my adolescent adoption of his brother – I was in danger of falling seriously in love.

Nicolas waited solicitously for me to pick up my knife and fork and take my first bite. 'All right?' he asked.

'Wonderful.' But I wasn't thinking about the food.

He topped up my glass. 'Of course,' he said judiciously, 'it'd cost the earth to get everything done at once. I think it would be a matter of doing things gradually, making the restoration of the house and grounds a lifetime's work.'

I nodded. My mouth was temporarily too much occupied with goose to allow me to give him my assurance that it was work that I would be only too happy to devote the rest of my life to, and this was just as well because born and bred and loves theatres and parties. She

'The thing is, though,' he said, taking up his own knife and fork with a wry smile, 'that Eve simply loathes the country.'

I stopped eating. 'Eve?'

'The girl I take out when I'm in London. She's city born and bred and loves theatres and parties. She works in advertising, but I think she'd dearly love to be an actress – I'm sure she'd envy you. Mmm, you're right, this goose *is* good.'

I put down my fork very slowly, and somehow managed to swallow the dust and ashes in my mouth. What a romantic idiot I'd been – of course Nicolas wasn't seriously interested in me. The attention he had been paying me was simply part of his job, something he could write off as expenses, a way of keeping my mind off the frightening task he had arranged for me tomorrow.

All my lightness had gone. I felt leaden, my head ached. The next-to-last thing I wanted to do was to eat the meal, but if I abandoned it now he would surely guess the reason. The very last thing I wanted was to talk about his girl-friend, but if I changed the subject abruptly, he might well begin to wonder why.

I sat up straight, took a sip of tasteless wine and picked up my fork again. 'Do tell me,' I begged, with a bright, sincere enthusiasm that my Drama School tutors would have been proud of, 'about Eve.'

Nicolas smiled and shrugged and reverted to his plans for the farm, but I soon abandoned all pretence of interest, as well as the remains of the goose. He tried to tempt me with strawberries and cream, but I managed to convince him that I wanted only black coffee. As soon as I had drunk it, I said I would like to go back to the hotel.

Nicolas protested. The evening had barely begun, he had wanted to take me to a night club, or perhaps to one of the open-air dance floors by the Havel. But I pleaded my headache, and he collected the car and drove me back towards Gatow.

I was silent on the journey. It had been pride that kept me bright at dinner, but by now I was too weary to bother about maintaining a façade. My interest in Nicolas had turned sour; this was no pleasure trip but business, and business of a frightening kind.

He glanced at me several times as we drove through the brightly-lit streets and out into the suburbs, and when we reached the quiet of a lakeside road he pulled up. It was not completely dark and the lake gleamed, catching the last light from the sky.

'Are you all right, Alison?' he asked gently.

'Yes, thank you,' I said, keeping my eyes on the tree-shadowed road ahead. 'I think it was the wine that gave me the headache – I was stupid to drink so much.'

He was contrite. 'I think it was much more likely my fault for insisting on staying at the pavement table. We must have been breathing petrol fumes all evening. You'd better get some fresh air before I take you back to the hotel.'

He held the door open and I stepped out on to the lakeside grass, reluctant to prolong the journey but glad of the opportunity to clear my head. The air was cool and fresh, smelling of waterweed and damp earth, but with an underlying fragrance that drifted towards us from a wild azalea whose flowers glimmered palely under the trees. From across the lake we could hear faintly the music of a restaurant band; the lights that hung about its landing stage were reflected in the water like a double string of pearls.

Nicolas took my arm and led me across the strip of grass towards the lake. There was a watery plop as a small creature took fright and dived in at our approach, and then we could hear only the distant music and the soft ripple and splash of the waves against the shingle bank.

He released my arm, bent to pick up a pebble and tossed it into the water. 'Don't think I don't understand,' he said quietly. 'You must be worried sick about tomorrow, you'd have no imagination at all if you weren't.' Then he turned to me quickly: 'But it'll be all right, Alison, truly – you'll probably find it simply rather boring.'

There was enough light for him to see whether I smiled, so I did my best. 'Pity I didn't bring my knitting, then.'

His reply was swift and sharp. 'For God's sake,

Alison, don't take *anything* of your own!' And then he relaxed again. 'But we've discussed all that. Sorry I missed your joke . . .'

He wandered a few feet away from me and bent to pick up another pebble. For a few moments he tossed it moodily in his hand, and then he leaned back and with a vicious gesture spun it far out into the lake. When he spoke it was half to himself, through partly-clenched teeth. 'I wish to heaven I'd never involved you in this! It seemed such a magnificent scheme at the time, when I saw how much you looked like Elisabeth. Oh, I was proud of my plan! But now . . . now I'd give anything to call it off. Not that it's difficult for you, but why should you be involved at all?'

I felt a moment of hope. 'Could you call it off?'

'Not a chance,' he said bitterly. 'I told you, I'm just an errand boy in this outfit. Anyway, there's too much at stake. By now Elisabeth is committed, and so are we.'

I shivered involuntarily, and he must have heard the catch in my breath. He came back to me, smiling with false heartiness, and put his hands on my shoulders. 'But look – what you're doing is really worthwhile, Alison, I promise you that. You're going to help Elisabeth spend more time with her grandmother, and that's a good humanitarian cause – right? And you're going to give a splendid performance, because you're a good actress. I know you'll have no problems – I'd never have brought you here if I hadn't been absolutely certain that you had the ability and the courage to go through with it.'

His hands were warm and strong. He smiled at me through the dusk, searching my features, moving his gaze from my eyes to my hair and my mouth and back again. And I knew that it was all part of the game, part of the plan he was proud of. Errand boy he might be, but an errand boy with ideas. 'That's all right, sir,' I could imagine him saying confidently to the man who gave out the orders, 'if the girl seems panicky I can always make love to her. They never fail to fall for that.'

I stiffened, standing mute and unwilling when he tried to draw me into his arms.

'What's wrong, Alison?' he said. 'I thought you liked me. I thought we'd established a rapport, out there on the lake this afternoon?'

I shrugged, trying to loosen the grip of his hands. 'Yes, I like you,' I said lightly, annoyed to hear that my voice was unsteady. 'That doesn't necessarily mean that I want to kiss you, though.'

For a moment I could hear only his breathing. 'No,' he said slowly, as though, with masculine arrogance, this possibility had never before occurred to him. 'No, I suppose it doesn't. But look, you're not holding back on account of Eve, are you? I mean, I'm not engaged to her, any more than you are to what's-his-name, the hairy fellow. All I was trying to tell you is that Eve doesn't fit into the kind of future that I want – I'm free to kiss whoever I like.'

The arrogance was intolerable. If my voice wavered this time, it was with anger. 'Always providing,' I pointed out, 'that she is prepared to kiss you.'

He raised an infuriatingly sceptical eyebrow. 'She was out on the lake this afternoon.'

'Then she has changed her mind.'

I thought for a moment that he would let me go. Then suddenly, his arms were tight about me and his mouth was hard against mine. I tried to disengage my lips, despising myself for the instinct that made me long to respond, telling myself that it was simply a chemical reaction and that I didn't want to pursue the experiment, and hating myself because I knew perfectly well that I did.

And then, as suddenly as he had begun, he stopped kissing me. He still held my arm, which was just as well because I was so shaken that I felt dizzy, but he drew away. 'I'm sorry,' he said unsteadily. 'That was selfish of me – you have a headache.'

I managed a shaky laugh. 'That hasn't done it much good.'

'I'm sorry,' he said again. 'I've been thinking about doing that ever since I saw you on the stage, and wanting to do it from the moment we met on the cliff-top. You were really magnificent then, Alison, when you thought that I was a hunted man who needed help and protection. I can't tell you how much I admired your courage and coolness and compassion. I have a very great regard for you, you know.'

Perhaps it was even true. But if so, he'd got my character all wrong; I wasn't in the least the kind of cool courageous person he needed for this job. It hadn't been courage that had put me back on his pony when I fell off, it had been a bid for his brother Simon's praise. It wasn't cool-headedness and compassion that had impelled me to try to help Nicolas on the cliff, but physical attraction. And if I now had to deny the attraction he had for me – as I must, because I knew that he was only using me and that after this episode I should probably never see him again – then there was nothing to sustain me at all.

He kissed me gently on the cheek, walked me back to the car, drove to the hotel and said a pleasant, friendly, good night.

The next morning at ten o'clock he was waiting, in his nondescript suit and plain German shirt and commonplace German car, to drive me on the first part of my illegal journey into East Berlin.

CHAPTER 9

The morning was grey and cool, more like November than May. Even the flowers in the gardens we passed looked subdued, matching my mood. I felt cold, despite my light sweater.

'Sleep well?' Nicolas enquired as we drove through the suburbs.

'Yes, thank you.'

He grinned at me from the corners of his eyes. 'Liar,' he observed pleasantly.

Well of course I was lying. I'd had a wretched night, tossing over and over as I went through his instructions in my mind and thought of further queries, further potential problems. And when I finally fell asleep I had dreamed vividly, waking in panic as I tried to run from some nameless dread towards Nicolas, a remote protector whose proffered hand I could never quite manage to reach . . .

I held myself stiffly, in an attempt to conceal my shivers. 'I will get a chance to talk to Elisabeth, won't I?' I asked, anxious to resolve one of the problems that had loomed hideously large in the night.

'I'm afraid not,' he said. 'Her absence from the East will be strictly timed and we can't risk any delay while you chat. Besides, she won't want to – her preoccupation is with her grandmother, remember.'

'Oh, but I *must* talk to her,' I cried. I drew a shaky breath and started again, trying to keep my voice from sounding as panicky as I felt.

'Look, Nicolas. I don't see how I'll ever get away with

pretending to be someone else – you can't do that kind of thing in real life. It doesn't matter how much alike Elisabeth and I may look, there will be a hundred obvious differences. Walk, gestures, voice, mannerisms . . . and if I can't even get an opportunity to talk to her there's no point in going through with it, because I'd be spotted immediately!'

'Of course you won't!' he said sternly. 'The only people you've got to deceive are the driver of the car, the East German guards at the checkpoint and the porter at the block of flats. As long as you're with Braun, they'll take your identity for granted. But I've arranged things at Elisabeth's grandmother's house so that you can watch her and listen to her as she goes in, and that should help. After all, you're a good actress.' He gave a friendly grin. 'What's the saying – "It'll be all right on the night"?'

All very well, for Nicolas; he'd be staying comfortably among the fleshpots of West Berlin while I was the one who risked arrest and imprisonment in the East. I glared at his profile, trying to tell myself that he was not in the least attractive, that I'd been a fool ever to think that he was, that he was really as dull and ordinary as his clothes and his choice of car suggested.

He went on talking, oblivious of my disapproval. 'I'm afraid I shan't be here when you come back tomorrow, but someone from the Department will be waiting for you. He'll take you back to Gatow and put you on the next flight out to England. Where do you want to go from Gatwick? Back to Norfolk?'

Tomorrow seemed unimaginably far ahead. 'Er – yes, I expect so. Yes of course, I'll have to be there when Aunt Madge gets back.'

'Right, I'll arrange for someone to meet you at Gatwick and drive you there. By tomorrow night you'll be safely back at your aunt's house.'

I nodded glumly. It was the thought of what I had to do in the intervening period that made me sick with worry.

'I'm due for some leave, as a matter of fact,' he went on. 'I intend to go back home at the end of the week and do some sailing – it'd be a good opportunity for you to start learning, if you'd like to?'

'I don't suppose I'll be staying in Norfolk beyond the weekend,' I said. 'Not after Aunt Madge gets back. Even if her car and the drive gates have been repaired, there's bound to be a bit of an atmosphere.'

He chuckled. 'All right then, come and stay at the farm. I know my mother would be happy to have you – and then I can show you over the empty house. I'd very much like you to see it.'

I murmured politely, declining to commit myself. It wasn't as though Nicolas really wanted to show me the house or entertain me at the farm or teach me to sail. He was merely doing his job, and trying to take my mind off the next twenty-four hours.

He had turned left off the busy main road that led towards the Brandenburg Gate, and was now driving through residential streets. The stucco façades of the older buildings were gashed and pock-marked. Despite the evident prosperity of West Berlin, the houses that had survived the bombs and shells of war still bore their scars.

Nicolas stopped beside a tall, solid nineteenth-century terraced house in a quiet street.

'Is this where Elisabeth's grandmother lives?'

'No – she's in the parallel street. It's just possible that her house may be watched, so we're taking a short cut through her cellar. Look, you see the man standing at the door over there?'

He was middle-aged, balding, shirt-sleeved, standing at the top of a short flight of steps and puffing a cigar while he glanced at a newspaper, and he gave us no sign of recognition or interest.

Nicolas checked his watch. 'That's George,' he said. 'He works for the Department and for the past two weeks he's been the tenant of the ground-floor apartment. He's the one who'll meet you as soon as you come back from East Berlin tomorrow. Ah, that's it, all clear.'

George had looked casually up and down the street, ground out his cigar butt, folded his newspaper and gone indoors. Nicolas waited for a minute, and then we followed and he rang the lowest bell.

George answered it immediately, and the men exchanged a laconic '*Guten Morgen*' as we stepped into the hallway. The introduction was brief: George gave me a nod and a smile, but I was too tense to return either. He opened an inner door, closed it behind us, and led us down some stairs and along a basement passage. At the far end, another door led to a windowless cellar that smelled of damp and of musty woodwork. When he flicked a switch a naked electric light bulb revealed an antiquated boiler, a heap of coal and a large gap newly knocked in the brickwork of the opposite wall.

'No problems?' Nicolas asked.

'None at all,' George confirmed. 'Should be a very smooth little operation.' He smiled at me, looking slightly bashful: 'Hope the shoes and things fitted?'

There had been a parcel waiting at the hotel for Nicolas when we arrived the previous afternoon. He had given it to me unopened when we said good night, telling me that the shoes and underclothes it contained were identical with Elisabeth's and that I must wear them today.

Poor Elisabeth! Or perhaps it wasn't her taste that was the problem, perhaps it was simply that attractive clothes weren't available in East Germany. Poor Elisabeth, either way! I'd looked in horror at the brand-new, hopelessly old-fashioned, grimly uncompromising underwear and at the boat-shaped casual shoes in an unattractive shade of light beige, and decided that there was such a thing as carrying authenticity too far. The shoes I'd have to wear, since they would be an essential part of her appearance, but what I wore underneath when I was on stage was strictly my own affair.

I smiled at George; no doubt he'd gone to a lot of

trouble to get the clothes. 'Yes, thank you,' I said sweetly. The shoes were a little sloppy, but that was the least of my worries.

He looked pleased. 'Fine. Good luck, then – and I'll be here waiting for you tomorrow.'

Nicolas ducked through the gap and held out his hand for me to follow him into the cellar of the house in the next street.

The light was already on; we were expected. The cellar was almost identical with the first, except that it was tidier and better stocked with fuel. Nicolas opened the door and we were immediately in another basement passage, at the end of which a woman was hovering to greet us.

She was tall, greying, somewhere in her mid-fifties, her shoulders a little stooped and her hands and voice tremulous with mingled fear, excitement and strain. 'Herr Allen?' she said, peering uncertainly. And then as Nicolas moved forward into the light she hurried to shake his hand. 'Yes of course, Herr Allen, I remember you well. And this is – ?'

Nicolas drew me forward. 'This is the young lady,' he said simply. To me he said: 'Frau Henschel is one of Elisabeth's aunts.'

As she saw me clearly for the first time Frau Henschel gave a nervous gasp, her hands flying up to her mouth, her eyes wide and apprehensive. And then she seized both my hands in hers and refused to let me go as she poured out her thoughts and emotions: how much I reminded her of her dead sister, Elisabeth's mother, how kind I was to help them, how brave I was to agree to take Elisabeth's place so that she could stay with them as long as possible. Her gratitude was embarrassing, but at the same time heart-warming. Whatever the deeper implications of the deception Nicolas had involved me in, I began for the first time to feel that I really was doing something genuinely useful for Elisabeth and her family.

With a prompt from Nicolas, who kept an eye on his

watch, I managed to disengage myself. Frau Henschel led us up the basement stair and into the main hall. This was still a one-family house and the hall was spotlessly clean, its black and white tiles newly washed and polished. There was an appetising smell of freshly-ground coffee, a welcome, I guessed, for Elisabeth. Frau Henschel was smartly dressed, but the agreeable aura of the perfumed toilet water she used could not quite mask the lingering smell of sick-room antiseptic.

'How is Elisabeth's grandmother?' I asked.

Frau Henschel shook her head sadly, glancing up the stairway, and I saw how tired and strained her eyes were. 'Only a matter of time,' she admitted wearily. 'A week perhaps.' But then she brightened.

'But Mother has been asking for Elisabeth. She will be so pleased to see her. She could not understand why the girl's visit had to be so brief, she forgets the Wall. And we dared not tell her Herr Allen's plan, because we did not really believe that you would be prepared to come.' She seized my hand again. 'We are so very grateful to you, my dear. It will mean so much to my mother.'

Nicolas, standing just beside me, put his arm lightly round my shoulders. I assured Frau Henschel that I was only too glad to help, and I hoped that it sounded sincere. I had begun to shiver again with nervous tension, and only the look of pride on Nicolas's face as he watched me, and the reassuring touch of his hand, kept me from bolting back down the basement stairs.

'Have you noticed anyone watching the house, Frau Henschel?' he asked.

She twisted her hands together. 'I think not, Herr Allen. But there has been so much work, so much worry with my mother . . . and now the excitement of Elisabeth's visit . . . '

He nodded understandingly. 'Never mind. But you will remember, won't you, that Elisabeth must change her clothes immediately, even before she sees her grandmother? This young lady must be ready to leave at exactly twenty minutes past the hour.'

Frau Henschel cut in eagerly. 'Yes, I remember your instructions. Everything is arranged.' She whirled nervously towards the front door, her hands fluttering to her lips again. 'I think I hear a car!' She strained to hear, then ran to the rear of the hall where there was a curtained-off lobby hung about with winter coats and scarves. 'This will be the best place for you to wait, Herr Allen.'

Nicolas drew me behind the curtain. 'I wanted you to be able to see as much as possible of Elisabeth,' he explained quietly, 'without either disturbing the family reunion or running the risk of being seen from the street when the door opens.'

Frau Henschel dithered, smoothing her hair and then her dress. Then she flung the door wide and, with a cry of joy, ran out and down the steps to greet her niece.

I waited tensely for my first sight of Elisabeth. In the space of a few minutes I would have to observe enough to enable me to give a convincing impersonation of her as I walked out of the door and into the official East German car. And if I made a hash of this part, it wouldn't be just a matter of going back to work as a waitress, it would be a matter of capture and punishment...

There was very little room in the lobby. Nicolas stood immediately behind me so that we could both look through the gap in the curtains. I could hear his steady breathing and feel the beat of his heart as his chest pressed against my shoulder. We said nothing, but the silence was alive and tingling.

And then there was a commotion. The door of an upper room opened and two other women came hurrying down the stairs, just as Frau Henschel came in through the front door with her arm triumphantly round a girl who had a light raincoat hanging loosely from her shoulders. There were glad cries and kisses and embraces, and I began to panic, jumping on my toes to try to catch a clear glimpse of Elisabeth.

'It's all right,' whispered Nicolas, his hands steadying me. 'Don't worry, they all know what's at stake.' And in a moment the other women retreated upstairs, and Frau Henschel firmly closed the front door.

My first reaction when I saw Elisabeth standing alone in the middle of the hall, was one of horrified disbelief. Nicolas must be out of his mind! He couldn't possibly expect me to impersonate this girl, we weren't in the least alike!

Elisabeth wore a pair of large dark-rimmed glasses. She was several inches taller than me and pounds heavier. The only similarity between us seemed to be that she was also wearing a pair of light beige boat-shaped shoes, and they were a good two sizes larger than mine.

I turned my head towards Nicolas, though I still kept my eyes on Elisabeth. 'We're completely different,' I hissed. 'I'll never get away with this!'

His hands tightened on my shoulders as he whispered against my hair, 'Yes you will. Just keep cool and watch her. Elisabeth doesn't wear glasses either, but Kurt provided her with a pair with plain lenses. As long as you're wearing them, no casual observer will notice the difference in your features. The raincoat slung over your shoulders will help conceal the fact that you're slimmer. And she's slightly round-shouldered, so she doesn't look that much taller than you. Now stop flapping, and concentrate.'

The man was a better observer than I was, I thought wryly; but then, no doubt the Department of Overseas Trade trained him for it. I was still tense, still frightened, but I forced myself to concentrate.

Elisabeth walked with quick, precise steps; she carried her handbag slung on a strap over her left forearm; she had a nervous habit of pushing up the bridge of her glasses with the second finger of her right hand, and then smoothing back her hair behind her right ear. Her face was devoid of make-up apart from lipstick, and she wore her hair combed straight back and caught in a knot at the nape of her neck. Her voice was light, but I almost smiled with relief as I heard the familiar Thuringian undertone. That at least was something I would have no problem with.

Elisabeth paused for a moment at the foot of the stairs, talking to her aunt, and then they moved up out of sight. At the same time, the man who had come in with her and had been standing quietly near the door now came forward. Nicolas pushed back the curtain and went out to meet him.

'Allen.'

'Braun.'

They introduced themselves and shook hands, looking at each other with interest. They were much of a height, though Braun was broader. He was perhaps ten years older than Nicolas, though his prematurely grey hair made his unlined face seem correspondingly younger so that it was difficult to assess his true age. His deep-set brown eyes had a wary, weary look, but he seemed genuinely glad to meet Nicolas.

'It's good to see you after so many years of faceless co-operation,' he said.

'Yes – I'm glad to have the chance of thanking you for it, particularly over this latest affair.' Nicolas drew me forward. 'This is Kurt Braun who will be looking after you. Braun, this is the new Elisabeth.'

I held out my hand. 'I'm Alison – ' I began, but Braun shook his head.

'Don't tell me,' he said. 'There is no need for me to know that.' He took my hand in a firm, brief grip. 'For me, you are Elisabeth Lorenz, the girl I came here with. You are really very much like her.'

'Everything all right on your side?' Nicolas asked.

'No problems at all,' Braun said confidently. Clearly he found it preferable to talk to Nicolas rather than to me. He was no charmer: uneasy, even a little shy with women, I guessed, a shyness that made him abrupt in manner. But his smile, when it came, was all the more pleasant.

'There will be no need for you to worry,' he told me. 'I'll bring you safely back to this house tomorrow. But now,' he turned again to Nicolas, 'I'd better rejoin my driver. As you know, we're suspicious on our side of the Wall. I am here to see that Elisabeth doesn't try to escape, the driver is here to make sure that I am doing nothing that has not been authorised, and now I must watch that he doesn't make a bolt for it himself. I shall be back to collect Elisabeth in – ' he checked his watch ' – exactly fifteen minutes.' He looked at me sternly, but with a hint of a smile. 'Please be sure that you are ready.'

Nicolas pulled me out of sight behind the curtain as Braun opened the front door, and then Frau Henschel came hurrying downstairs carrying a pile of clothes.

'You can change in here,' she said breathlessly, opening a door that led to a small cloakroom. 'I hope you will find everything that you need.'

The room was lighted by a window of frosted glass, and the fittings were solidly old-fashioned. The water came boiling from serpentine pipes, and there was a clean towel, a fresh cake of soap, a box of tissues, a packet of hairpins and a clutch of safety-pins beside the wash-basin. Frau Henschel – or perhaps the Department of Overseas Trade – seemed to have thought of everything.

I pulled off my sweater, stepped out of my skirt and cleaned all traces of make-up from my face. Elisabeth's clothes consisted of the raincoat, a brown skirt and a plain cotton blouse in a disagreeable shade of yellow. The skirt came just to my knees, so it must have been very short on her. It was loose at the waist and hips, but I hitched it as securely as possible with the safety-pins.

I scraped back my hair and twisted and pinned it into place at the nape of my neck, and then examined Elisabeth's – now my – handbag. It contained very little: an identity card, a purse with a small quantity of East

German marks and a return railway ticket to her home in Thuringia, her fake glasses, her watch, a clean handkerchief, a comb and a lipstick.

I unscrewed the brown plastic case of the lipstick. It was new and unused – sweet of her to think of that – but the texture looked unpleasantly greasy. And I hated the colour, a trying shade of purplish red that wouldn't suit me, or Elisabeth, or our yellow blouse in the least.

No, there were limits. What I needed was confidence, and I couldn't step outside feeling confident if I wore that dreadful colour, any more than if I'd been wearing the fibreglass East German underwear. I rummaged in my own handbag, found and applied my own lipstick. No one would be able to remember what colour Elisabeth had been wearing.

That cheered me up a little. I slipped my own lipstick as well as hers into Elisabeth's bag, then put on her watch and adjusted her fake glasses. They tended to slip so I practised her gesture of pushing them up with the second finger of my right hand, and then smoothing my hair into place behind my ear.

There was a knock at the door. 'Ready, Alison?'

I gulped, and took a final glimpse in the mirror. It was exactly like hearing the last call before going on stage. I was trembling with nerves and feeling cold and sick. I had to forcc my fcct into motion to gct me through the door.

Nicolas was waiting, his face anxious, but it lit with a wide smile as he saw me.

'Oh, that's wonderful, Alison! You've done a magnificent job. Really, I'd hardly know the difference!'

I managed a hollow smile. He'd have to say that, anyway; it was too late to change anything, and he'd know how important it was for me to feel confident.

He held me at arm's length. 'Mind you,' he said with a grin, 'I much prefer the original Alison. Just make sure you change back before I see you again – in Norfolk at the weekend, remember? I'm looking forward to that.'

I nodded wanly and at that moment the doorbell rang. Frau Henschel hurried downstairs to let Kurt Braun in and then, as she turned and saw me, she let out a gasp of surprise and anxiety.

'My dear,' she said, running to take my hands between her, 'my dear, you look so much like Elisabeth – and you are so very brave. All our good wishes and thanks go with you . . .'

'Ready?' Braun cut in.

'In a minute,' Nicolas snapped.

Frau Henschel's hands fluttered, and still murmuring her thanks and good wishes she retreated up the stairs. Nicolas took Elisabeth's raincoat from my arm and placed it round my shoulders, then turned me gently to face him.

'I believe that all good actors have first night nerves,' he said. 'But once they're on stage they're too much absorbed in their part to think of anything else – am I right?'

'I – I believe so.'

'Well, then . . . you'll have no worries. Good luck, Alison.'

His hands tightened on my shoulders. 'See you in Norfolk,' he murmured, and then he bent to kiss me lightly on the cheek, taking care not to disarrange my hair or lipstick. Then he straightened.

'All right, Braun, she's ready. But for God's sake take care of her, do you hear?'

Kurt Braun was impatient. 'I will, of course. She'll have no trouble. But we must leave now.'

Nicolas released me and smiled. '*Auf wiedersehen*, then, Alison – until we see each other again . . .'

The time had come to step on to the stage. I took the three slow deep breaths that always help to relax and steady me before the ordeal of appearing in public. Then I pushed the glasses up on to the bridge of my nose, smoothed back my hair, slung Elisabeth's bag over my left forearm and, stepping quickly and precisely, followed Kurt Braun out of the door and down the steps and into the black East German car that was waiting to take me through the Berlin Wall.

CHAPTER 10

The engine was already running and the driver seemed impatient to be off. He glanced incuriously at me as I got in, but as soon as the back doors were closed he set the car moving.

It would have been unnatural to drive in complete silence: 'And how was your grandmother, Comrade?' asked Braun.

I started, shocked by the unexpectedness of the form of address as much as by the question, but then I recalled that I had asked Frau Henschel the same thing. 'She is very ill,' I replied quietly. 'Only a matter of time now.'

He assumed an air of officious satisfaction. 'Then it's fortunate for you that these arrangements could be made, isn't it? You must make the most of your second visit, tomorrow.'

His tone had a dismissive hint making it clear that he had no wish to prolong the conversation, and I was relieved. I didn't think that I would be able to address him as 'Comrade' without sounding as self-conscious as I felt, so the less I had to say and the less I drew attention to myself, the better. Besides, no one would expect a girl who had just visited her dying grandmother to be chatty.

Braun spoke again, addressing the back of the driver's head: 'An unimpressive area this, Comrade Felsen.'

The driver agreed. 'These old terraces should have been pulled down long ago to make way for workers' flats. West Berlin has no charms for me, I can tell you.'

I listened with wry amusement as they made a point of out-doing each other in condemnation of all things Western, ignoring everything that was attractive and prosperous and eagerly drawing each other's attention to the slightest evidence of decay or neglect. And then my stomach tightened as the great grey barrier of the Wall loomed at the end of the street.

I had assumed that we should be going through the famous Checkpoint Charlie but that, Nicolas told me, was the crossing-point for foreigners. West and East German nationals used one of the two other crossing-points in the centre of the city. We turned a corner, joined a main road, and there ahead of us, just as at any frontier between two different countries, were striped barriers manned by border police.

The driver stopped at the West German barrier. The green-uniformed police glanced at the driver's papers and waved us through. They might perhaps have been tempted to search a private East German car for smuggled goods, but they knew an official car when they saw it and took care not to provoke a political incident.

The car rolled forward to the heavy, crash-proof East German barrier, and two grey-uniformed East German guards armed with rifles came up on either side of us. They too recognised the official car, but this seemed to make them even more zealous in their duties. Braun handed them a sheaf of papers, we all passed over our identity cards, and one of the guards took them into the guardhouse. The other stayed with us, hitching his slung rifle higher on his shoulder. Our driver switched off his engine, and we sat and waited.

Even the driver seemed subdued. Kurt Braun made an attempt at jocular conversation through the car window with the guard but the man was wooden, refusing to commit himself even on the state of the weather. As for me, my mouth was dry with fear and I had great difficulty in stopping myself from trembling visibly.

This scrutiny of our papers was nonsense. The car had been through the checkpoint only half an hour previously, and no problem over our papers could possibly have arisen in that time . . . unless . . .

Unless of course, they had any reason to think that a switch had been made. And if they had such a reason, if they had the slightest suspicion that anything was wrong, this was the point where it would all start to happen.

This was where I would be asked to get out of the car and go into the guardhouse for questioning, and if I were questioned I should be lost. I'd try to bluff it out, of course, to maintain for as long as possible that I really was Elisabeth in the hope that they would believe me and let me go. Nicolas had told me enough of her background to enable me to keep up a convincing initial performance.

But my German would never stand up to skilled questioning. They would break my story with very little trouble, and then the fact that I had lied to them would almost certainly make it worse for me . . . I might get ten years in prison, not five!

Oh God, what a mess I was in . . . what a mess I'd let Nicolas get me into! I could feel that my hands were damp with perspiration, despite the fact that I was cold.

A telephone in the guardhouse rang with shrill insistence. I started. From the corner of my eye I saw Kurt Braun watching me covertly, anxiously, his spread hand hovering close to mine in mute warning.

An officer came from the guardhouse, hitching at the belt which held his revolver. He had the papers in his hand, and after glancing at Braun and the driver he came round to where I sat and motioned me to open the window.

Then he put one elbow on it, frowned at the photograph on Elisabeth's identity card and peered hard at me from a distance of no more than eighteen inches. I tried not to flinch. He was about thirty, tall and podgy, with fleshy red lips under a small dark moustache, and his breath smelled foully of schnapps.

'Comrade Elisabeth Lorenz,' he read out slowly. 'From Eisenach.'

I tried to loosen my hands from each other's grasp so as to hide the betraying whiteness of the knuckles. 'That's right, Comrade,' I heard myself murmur.

He gave a swaggering laugh. 'A little Thuringian up to see the sights of the big city, eh?'

'To visit my sick grandmother,' I corrected him quickly.

He thumbed through the papers. 'Ah yes, two compassionate visits to the West, one today and one tomorrow. And how did you like it over there, eh?'

I forced myself to meet his eyes. After all, the real Elisabeth would have had good cause for looking wretched. 'My grandmother is dying,' I told him.

'Oh yes?' His voice was indifferent, entirely devoid of compassion. He looked again at Elisabeth's identity card and then at me, his tongue flicking wetly over his lips as his eyes roamed. 'Well, we'll see you tomorrow, then?'

'Yes . . . Comrade.'

'Right.' He tossed the papers to one of the guards and sauntered away, an urban bully-boy showing off to a girl from the country. The guard thrust the papers back through the open window to Braun, and the barriers were lifted to let us through. I expelled a shuddering breath.

And had that pig of an officer, I wondered, biting my lips as I remembered the discrepancy, noticed that although Elisabeth had been described on her identity card as having grey eyes, mine were most definitely blue?

And if he hadn't spotted it today, would he tomorrow?

*

The driver was voluble with relief as he accelerated away. He hated going to the West, it was nothing but trouble. And the traffic! He'd much rather stay in the

DDR, where driving was still a pleasure instead of a problem.

He had a point, I could see that. The area we were passing through, just to the east of the Wall, was almost completely empty: of traffic, of buildings, of people. Once it had been the heart of a great city, and now it was a wasteland, with the ruins of a few major buildings still in crumbling evidence as though the war had finished within the last decade instead of in 1945. The car window was still open and when we stopped at an intersection I could hear the silence of desolation.

But then, away from the Wall and among the streets, the city began to come to life; as though the old centre was a back yard that had been deliberately abandoned. The traffic thickened, though to nothing like the same extent as in West Berlin, and there were more people about. But as I watched and gathered my impressions I realised that whatever it might have been originally, the Wall was no longer a barrier between two halves of the same city.

The vehicles here were different from those on the other side of the Wall. The traffic signs were different. The clothes were different. The street lights were different. The uniforms of officialdom were different. East Berlin was the capital city of another country.

A country where the laws were different, too. And I was here illegally, with someone else's identity card, and only the man beside me could get me out again.

I looked at him nervously, speculatively. Nicolas had told me that he didn't know whether I would like Kurt Braun, but that I could certainly trust him. Yes, I felt that instinctively.

He saw me watching him, and his eyes showed me his relief that we had managed to get through the checkpoint safely. Then, taking advantage of the driver's preoccupation with a traffic roundabout, he gave me a slow, shy, friendly smile.

My spirits lifted. I thought that I might very well find myself liking him too.

Now that we were in the heart of East Berlin, Kurt became more expansive, pointing out the sights to the girl supposedly up from the country. We went along the Unter den Linden, where the trees were still small but definitely flourishing and the pavement cafés, though fewer than in the Ku'damm, seemed to be doing a brisk trade. And then he said, 'And here we are, back again in Lenin Allee,' and I guessed that I had reached the end of my journey.

Lenin Allee was enormous in every sense: a tremendously wide straight avenue with central flower beds, wide roadways and wide pavements, and on either side, block after monolithic block of apartment buildings, with stores at ground level. About half-way along, when the buildings at either end were lost in the mile-long distance, the driver pulled up and Kurt motioned me to get out.

'Here at ten-thirty tomorrow then, Comrade Felsen, if you please?' he said politely to the driver, who nodded grudgingly, slammed the door shut and drove off, leaving us alone on the wide pavement.

'We mustn't stand talking here,' Kurt said quickly. 'It might attract attention. There's just the porter, a woman, by the way, to deal with now. Please ask me, in front of her, to join you for a cup of coffee, so that I can show you where your apartment is. We can talk there.'

We walked together across the pavement and entered a door. Beside a desk in the entrance hall, a dumpy middle-aged woman sat knitting. As we came in she glanced up, and for a moment her needles froze in motion as she stared at us, her pale blue eyes shrewd and unsmiling.

'Back again, Comrade,' Kurt announced heartily.

For a moment I held my breath, and then let it out again as the needles resumed their clacking. 'Ah yes,' said the woman. 'Comrade Lorenz, who is staying in the apartment of Ilse Schmidt, am I right? So many tenants, you know, but I rarely forget a face for more than a few seconds. Now let me see – a compassionate visit to the West, isn't it?'

I nodded. 'My grandmother is dying.'

The porter stilled her needles for a moment and clicked her tongue sympathetically. 'Well, well . . . a good age, I dare say?'

I had no idea, but it seemed a safe bet. 'A great age,' I agreed.

She sighed robustly. 'Well, there, we all have to go some time. A big advantage for you, Comrade Lorenz, to be able to visit her – and to be allowed to use one of these fine apartments while you're in East Berlin! I hope you appreciate your good fortune.'

I suppressed an instinctive retort that in any right-minded country a girl would be free to visit her relatives at any time, and stay as long as she wished.

'Oh, yes I do,' I assured her quickly. 'It's a beautiful apartment – and now I'm looking forward to making myself some coffee.' I turned to Kurt. 'Would you care to join me – er – Comrade?'

He made a business of frowning at his watch. 'Well . . . perhaps one quick cup – thank you.'

I nodded pleasantly at the porter who looked at me impassively over her clicking needles, and Kurt led me towards a lift. There was one other passenger in it, and we rode to the top floor in silence. The long corridor was empty, but Kurt put a warning finger to his lips and I followed him silently to a door numbered 6327. He took a key from his pocket, threw the door open and announced heartily: 'Safely back again then, Comrade. Kind of you to invite me for coffee. I'd appreciate that . . . Splendid apartment, isn't it? I very much admire the view . . .'

Talking all the time he crossed the bed-sitting-room to the tiny kitchen, turned the cold tap full on and left it splashing water loudly into the sink.

He made no move to fill the kettle and for a moment I stared at him incredulously. Why on earth leave a tap running?

But I'd watched thrillers on television, hadn't I? I'd watched the news, and documentaries. I knew that in cold fact, as well as in fiction, hotel rooms and offices could be bugged. I also knew that by creating a background of noise it was possible to prevent the listening devices from picking up conversations.

So the apartment that Elisabeth had been loaned for her visit, while its owner was on holiday, was bugged. She was being spied on. But why? Why did the East German officials let her go to the West at all, if they wanted to check on her as closely as that?

Not that the reasons need concern me. It didn't matter a *pfennig* to me *why* they wanted to listen to her conversations. The fact was that if they were doing so, if they really were checking on her that closely, I hadn't a hope of getting away with my deception.

CHAPTER 11

I followed Kurt to the kitchen. He must have noticed my shocked look, because he gave me one of his rare, reassuring smiles.

'This is probably not necessary,' he said, close to my ear. 'But one never knows. It's always best to take routine precautions.'

I felt relieved. Perhaps I was worrying for nothing, perhaps Elisabeth wasn't being watched at all. But Kurt's matter-of-fact acceptance that anyone's apartment might be bugged was, I found, distinctly chilling.

He went back to the sitting-room, hunted for and found a transistor radio, and turned it to music. Then he stood in the kitchen doorway, looking at me with slightly embarrassed approval.

'You have done very well indeed,' he said. 'You were utterly convincing. But then, I believe that you are an actress? Frankly, when I had a message from Allen to say that he knew a girl who would be able to take Elisabeth's place so that she could stay longer in the West, I was sceptical. But he insisted that you would be perfect in every way, and now I know that he was right.'

'Thank you – but I'm not too happy about it,' I said glumly. 'That officer at the checkpoint – '

'Yes, that was an awkward moment. I was ready to deal with any official questioning, but I was not prepared for an officer who took a fancy to you! He wasn't on duty when I took Elisabeth through, and we must hope that he won't be there tomorrow. But really, you dealt with him splendidly. Half your task is done now, so you can relax. I'm afraid that you will probably find it very dull here on your own until tomorrow.'

'That's what Nicolas said. Still,' I glanced round the room, 'there are books, television, the radio – I shall be able to pass the time. Would you really like some coffee, by the way? It seems a pity to waste all that water.'

'Please don't bother – it will help to occupy your time when I've gone.' He looked at me thoughtfully. 'You are an old friend of Allen, I believe?'

'We knew each other as children. We haven't met for years, though.'

'But now that you have met again, your friendship has resumed?' He tried some jocular gallantry. 'Don't deny it, I could see that for myself!'

I knew that my colour was rising. 'I like him very much.'

'And he finds you very attractive. Well, this means that there will be a happy ending to this adventure of yours. I'm sure he will be waiting anxiously for your return tomorrow.'

'Well, he won't actually . . .'

I hesitated. Although Kurt was a man I could trust, Nicolas had so insistently drummed into my head the 'need to know' principle that I instinctively stopped myself from blurting out the fact that Nicolas wouldn't be waiting for me because he had another job to do. I coloured again, knowing that even those few words, coupled with my awkward stumble into silence, had already given far too much away.

But Kurt came immediately to my rescue. 'Please don't think that I was trying to test you!' he protested, smiling. 'Though I'm glad to see that Allen has trained you well – but that's understandable. He has an excellent reputation and a bright career ahead of him, I'm sure of that.'

'Has he?' Ridiculously, considering the shortness of the time we had spent together, I felt strange without Nicolas by my side; almost as though I had lost a limb. I found myself eager to discuss him, in compensation.

'He doesn't talk about his job, of course,' I went on, choosing my words with care, 'except to grumble about being used as an errand boy.'

'He's a little more than that, I assure you! We've worked in co-operation on several occasions, and I've always been most impressed by him. That's why I was so glad to have the opportunity to meet him today for the first time.'

'He doesn't come to East Berlin, then?'

'Not to my knowledge. His work is in the West, screening East Germans who ask for political asylum. Oh, I imagine that he knows East Berlin, but there are people on this side who would very much like to get their hands on him, so if he comes here he does it very quietly. A professionally inconspicuous man, your friend Nicolas Allen!'

Kurt looked at his watch. 'I have to go now. I think you will find that Elisabeth has left you everything that you will need. If you want exercise, by all means stroll to the end of the block, but otherwise please stay quietly here. Oh, and don't let that porter involve you in conversation, she's a gossip – and worse.'

'Worse?'

He shrugged. 'These are government apartments and she's a government employee. You might say that it's part of her job to gossip . . . But as Elisabeth Lorenz who has just visited her dying grandmother, you have a perfect excuse for being uncommunicative. Don't forget that, will you?'

Kurt turned off the tap and lowered the volume of the radio.

'Thank you so much for the coffee, Comrade,' he said clearly. 'Until tomorrow morning, then – please be ready at ten twenty-five exactly.'

He handed me the key of the apartment and smiled, the shyness lifting from his brown eyes. Then, in the old German fashion, he took my hand and bowed over it stiffly before letting himself out.

I watched him go, and as I did so I knew exactly

what had been subconsciously bothering me about the way he was dressed.

His clothes reminded me strangely of the clothes that Nicolas had worn.

Not in colour, material or age. Kurt was wearing a plain grey town suit, made of some kind of ersatz worsted; from the sharpness of the creases it looked almost new, though the quality of the cloth would never stand up to the kind of wear that Nicolas's suit had weathered. No, the similarity between their clothes was in the cut.

That was it, of course! The clothes of the East Berliners had been conspicuously different from those of the West because of a time-lag in fashion. In terms of fashion, crossing the Wall had set me back years. The girls in the East were wearing mini-skirts, the men narrow trousers.

Kurt's new suit had narrow trousers; so had Nicolas's old suit.

In fashion-conscious West Berlin, the cut of Nicolas's suit had made him look drably outdated. That might even have been why he preferred to eat at a pavement restaurant, rather than go indoors under the brighter lights. But if he came over here, to East Berlin, there would be nothing remarkable about his appearance at all . . .

What was it Kurt had said? ' . . . A professionally inconspicuous man, your friend Mr Allen . . . '

And what had Nicolas said at the restaurant last night when he was telling me about his job? Something about it being a good career – as long as you remembered to keep a low profile.

And then . . . then he'd said something about being used for target practice.

I hadn't had the sense to see it at the time. I'd been too worried about my impersonation of Elisabeth, and I'd even thought bitterly of Nicolas enjoying himself in West Berlin while I was in danger in the East. Instead of that, he was almost certainly coming here himself –

possibly he was here already, somewhere out on the streets of East Berlin, where Kurt had said there were people who wanted to get their hands on him.

Or, as he'd said himself, people who wanted to use him for target practice.

Nicolas was in far greater danger than I was. And in the moment when I realised it I found myself forced to acknowledge that – even though he had another girl-friend, even though I knew that he was simply making use of me – the sick sensation of anguish in my heart was occasioned quite simply by love.

*

The day dragged.

I made myself some coffee, then wandered round the apartment looking at books and newspapers and came to the conclusion that Ilse Schmidt, whose home it was, was a teacher of mathematics and an enthusiastic member of the East German Communist Party.

Then I had lunch. Elisabeth had kindly shopped for me before she left, and I found butter, cheese and eggs in the refrigerator, bread and apples in the cabinet. She herself had left hardly any traces of her occupation, except for the suitcase beside the bed, and I wondered how she had passed the time in the confines of the room.

After I had eaten, washed up everything I could find and cleaned the sink meticulously, I could bear the inactivity no longer and decided to go out for a walk. I patted my hair into place, slung Elisabeth's raincoat round my shoulders and went down to the entrance hall. Fortunately the porter was busy with a tenant who was complaining volubly about a blocked sink and I was able to walk past without being involved in conversation, but her sharp eyes swivelled as I passed. There was no doubt that she missed very little.

The straight lines and depressingly solid architecture of Lenin Allee made it an unexciting place for a walk. I would very much have preferred to explore the more interesting parts of East Berlin – but not in the persona of Elisabeth Lorenz. Kurt had advised me to go no further than the end of the block, and that was exactly what I did. And as I walked, conscious all the time that East Berlin was an alarmingly *foreign* foreign city, I tried to imagine that Nicolas, in his inconspicuous suit, was somewhere near, keeping a friendly eye on me.

It was foolish to imagine that he might be in Lenin Allee, of course. It would have been pointless activity for him to watch over me, a waste of his professional time. But at least it took my mind off the uneasy possibility that my movements might be watched by anyone else.

Trying to remember that I was Elisabeth Lorenz from Thuringia, in the city for perhaps the first time, I made a point of slowing my pace on the way back and lingering to look in the windows of the stores. The displays were attractive, but there was none of the quantity, the frivolity, the quality, the variety, the extravagance that I had seen in the stores of West Berlin.

I ran almost gaily up the steps of the apartment block, thinking of my return to the West, and England, and Nicolas. The porter, presiding over nothing but her knitting, looked up at me with disapproval.

'You've enjoyed your walk, Comrade?'

I sobered, remembering that I had momentarily forgotten my rôle. 'Oh – oh yes, very much. I enjoy looking at the shop windows.'

Her thick fingers deftly whirled the wool over her flashing needles. 'But they're not as good as those in the West, I dare say?'

I must have crimsoned. It had been madness for me to allow my guard to drop in public, even for a moment. Did she *know* that I wasn't Elisabeth? Was she just guessing? Or did she believe that I was Elisabeth, but suspect me of planning to defect tomorrow?

'I – er – I really don't know, Comrade,' I stammered. 'I simply visited my grandmother's house – I didn't see any of the stores.'

Her fingers still flew, but her gaze was fixed unwaveringly on my face. I couldn't read what was in it: disbelief? suspicion? contempt?

'And you drove through the West with your eyes shut?' she said mockingly.

'No, I didn't, of course not . . . but my grandmother lives in a residential district, there are no big shops there at all, nothing to compare with Lenin Allee . . . '

'Hmmm. I'd have expected you to take more notice than that, a girl like you. Aren't you curious about the West, then?'

'Oh, I'm perfectly happy in Eisenach, I assure you.' I began to move crab-wise towards the lift. 'I've no wish to go anywhere else.'

The porter turned a row and laughed sceptically. 'That's not what my poor cousin Herta says about Eisenach! She married a butcher from the town – a dreary hole, she says it is, though anywhere would be dreary tied to a boorish husband like that. I can't think why she married him. Never did like the Thuringians myself . . . no offence to you, Comrade, of course, but I knew your accent right away. "Here comes one of poor cousin Herta's fellow-countrywomen," I said to myself when you arrived yesterday, and then it turns out that you come from the very same town!'

I edged as far as the lift and pressed the button hard. 'Yes, well . . . ' I said awkwardly, 'you feel differently about a place when you're born and bred in it, don't you?' I pressed the button again, urgently.

The needles clacked on. 'I suppose you do,' the porter conceded. 'Then I'm sure you must know Eisenach like the back of your hand, eh? I expect you'll know my cousin's husband's shop, corner of Finkelstrasse and Bahnhofstrasse? Walter Schinken, butcher – that was his father's name, a very old-established business in the town. You must know it, I'm sure?'

Was it a trap? I swallowed painfully, trying to keep a smile tacked on to my face as I leaned against the bell and prayed for the lift to come. What an idiot I'd been to stray from the security of my room! And Kurt had warned me about the porter, yet I had still allowed her to talk me into this untenable position. If the shop existed, presumably Elisabeth would know it – but suppose it didn't exist, suppose the woman was deliberately trying to trick me . . . ?'

'I – er – I'm not quite sure – ' I began, hedging desperately. It had been all very well for Nicolas to say that as an actress I was ideal for this job, but I was used to working from scripts. And here I was, right in the middle of the terrifying nightmare that comes recurrently to all actors: alone in the centre of the stage with an expectant audience and no idea of the plot, let alone of my words.

Only this time I wasn't dreaming, and the audience wouldn't catcall or give me a slow handclap, and it certainly wouldn't get up and walk out.

Instead, it put down its knitting.

I looked desperately at the main door. If only this were a play, Nicolas would come bursting in to my rescue.

And at that moment, dead on cue, the door did indeed swing open, to admit an elderly postman who grumbled about his fallen arches as he hobbled across to the desk to slap down a pile of letters.

I had never seen anyone quite so beautiful. I beamed at him, slipped into the lift which had just bumped to a halt, pressed the button for the sixth floor and scuttled back to the safety of my burrow.

For a few moments after I had slammed and locked the door behind me, I leaned on it and shivered. The experience had shaken me even more than the crossing of the Wall, because at least Kurt had been with me there. I was angry with myself for my folly, and terrified that the porter would be sufficiently suspicious of me to come and make further enquiries. I forced myself to act naturally and make and drink a cup of coffee, but for every moment of the next hour I expected a knock to come at the door.

It didn't, and gradually I relaxed. Of course the porter wasn't trying to trap me, she was merely gossiping about her cousin to pass the time. I listened to a concert on the radio, made myself a cheese omelette for supper, watched some beautifully-controlled ballet-like gymnastics on television, and decided to have an early night.

Elisabeth had gone to considerable trouble on my behalf, making up the bed with clean linen and even laying out for me a clean, chaste – not to say unalluring – nightie. I very much missed my hairbrush and toothbrush, but I took a bath and rubbed some of her gritty paste on my teeth with my finger, and then washed out my undies and spread them to dry on the towel rail. I was extremely glad that I had kept my own: cheap they may have been, but at least they were cheerful – St Michael at his most herbaceous.

Tomorrow, I thought as I lay awake for a few moments, tomorrow this will be all over. There will just be the trip back through the Wall with Kurt, and then the moment I'm back in Elisabeth's grandmother's house I can pick up my own life again. Nicolas's friend George will meet me in the cellar, and then I'll be taken back to Norfolk with no more worry or effort on my part.

And at the weekend Nicolas will be home at the farm, and he couldn't not come to see me, not after all I've done. And we'll go sailing, and he'll show me the Georgian house he wants to live in and . . . and after that, who knows?

I felt content to leave it at that, and fell asleep.

I slept well, almost dreamlessly, and woke happy. There was a serviceably plain wrap hanging behind the bathroom door, either Elisabeth's or Ilse Schmidt's, and I slipped it on while I pottered about making coffee and tidying the flat.

Kurt was due at ten twenty-five. There was still a quarter of an hour to go when I heard the knock, and I still hadn't dressed, but I was so eager to start the journey back that I ran to open the door immediately.

It wasn't Kurt.

Instead, two men in grey suits and trilby hats stood looking at me impassively.

'Comrade Elisabeth Lorenz?' said the thin dark one.

My hand went nervously up to my lips. I nodded.

'We have some sad news for you. May we come in?'

They advanced without waiting for my agreement and I found myself backing clumsily into the sitting-room.

'News . . . ?' I heard myself saying, my voice cracking with tension.

'Yes. I am sorry to have to tell you that your grand-mother died last night. You will not need to go to West Berlin today after all, Comrade.'

CHAPTER 12

I swayed. I could feel the blood draining from my cheeks, leaving them pinched and cold. 'But – ' I stammered, ' – but – '

The spokesman took off his hat, revealing a prematurely balding head. His dark face was thin, his nose and eyes sharp. He watched me like a bird of prey, waiting for my reaction.

My mind was in a turmoil. I was near to panic, the implication of his words filling me with blind terror, and only my stage training kept me from breaking down.

The show had to go on. At all costs, I had to remember my rôle. I wasn't Alison Maxwell who was desperate to get back to the safety of the West, I was Elisabeth Lorenz who had just heard that her much-loved grandmother had died.

Or had she really died? Did they suspect the switch? Had they come to test my story?

I sagged into an armchair and bent my face down on my hands, playing for enough time to think my way through this terrifying situation. Alone, I would be helpless; I might as well confess and get it over. But Kurt would arrive within the next ten minutes, and he would be able to extricate me. Yes, I was sure of that. Nicolas had trusted Kurt and put me in his care, and he would know what to do.

In the meantime I had to try to react as Elisabeth would have done. I looked up at the men, my eyes, my face, my voice all showing the grief that she would feel.

'But – oh, but surely my grandmother can't be dead?'

I appealed to the man. 'The doctor said yesterday that it might be a week – she can't have gone so quickly.'

He shrugged, politely regretful. 'I understand that she was very old. A sudden relapse, I imagine.'

'How do – how did you hear this, Comrade?'

'We have very reliable sources of information.'

'I see . . . ' I stood up, clutching the borrowed wrap round me, and faced him with dignity. 'I would still like to go to West Berlin today, please, to pay my respects and comfort my aunt.'

He raised his eyebrows, making his face even longer and thinner. 'That is not within the terms of your permit, Comrade. You were allowed to make two visits to the West for the purpose of seeing your grandmother when she was gravely ill. Her death invalidates that permit.'

The callousness of East German officialdom appalled me, but anger would not be in character; presumably Elisabeth understood the system. 'Comrade Braun will be here in a few minutes,' I said. 'I will ask him when he arrives – I'm sure he will be able to arrange it.'

The man gave a thin smile. 'Comrade Braun would have been here,' he corrected me, 'but when the news of your grandmother's death came, his instructions were cancelled.'

I sat down again. I hadn't much option; my knees seemed suddenly to give way. If Kurt wasn't allowed to come, then I really was on my own.

'But I *must* go back,' I babbled, finding no difficulty at all in making my voice break with tears, because they were so nearly genuine. 'My relatives are expecting me to go back. You can't stop me now, it would be too cruel! Oh please, just for twenty minutes –'

He shook his head implacably. 'Your permit has been withdrawn,' he said. 'You know as well as I do, Comrade, how difficult it was to get the permit in the first place. Oh, not because of your own record, that has always been impeccable. But your father has been a trouble-maker.'

I remembered what Nicolas had told me about Elisabeth's background. 'My poor father is in hospital,' I retorted.

'*Now* he is. Lucky for him that he had a nervous illness, or he might well have found himself on trial as an enemy of the State. It was his record that made the authorities so reluctant to grant you your permit, Comrade. But they were generous. You should be grateful that you were able to see your grandmother at all. There is nothing more that you can do over there now.'

'But – but the funeral,' I stammered, clutching at fronds of hope. 'I must go to the funeral.'

He exchanged an exasperated glance with his companion, a stocky blond young man who had been quietly and systematically searching the bed-sitting-room during our conversation. 'You have no permit to attend a funeral in West Berlin,' he pointed out. 'That would have to be applied for separately.'

I looked up hopefully and for a moment he seemed anxious to help. 'In the circumstances,' he went on, 'it might quite well be granted. Yes,' he fingered his blue-black chin thoughtfully, 'I should think you might very well have a good case for attending the funeral.'

My hopes and knees strengthened. I stood up.

A smile hovered on the man's thin mouth. 'Unfortunately, however,' he added, 'permits to the West take rather a long time to come through. You know this from your own experience, Comrade. How long was it before you got your permit for the compassionate visit – three weeks, a month? I doubt if your grandmother could wait so long for her funeral.'

I turned away, trembling, disgusted by his sick joke. Dear heaven, what would happen to me now?

What a hideous predicament Nicolas had put me in! He had been so confident, so reassuring about the simplicity of this switch – and now I was in deep trouble, and entirely on my own.

Except . . . except that Nicolas was probably here, somewhere in East Berlin. My spirits lifted a little. Kurt would know what had happened to me and surely he would be able to get in touch with Nicolas. Between them they were certain to rescue me.

I faced the men again, holding my head high. All I could do now was to co-operate with them while I waited for help to arrive. They had given me no indication that they thought that I was not the real Elisabeth; perhaps their story was true, perhaps they really had come to break the news of her grandmother's death and her cancelled permit. If I kept my head and did as they wanted, there was no reason why they should suspect me at all.

'What – ' I heard my voice rise with nervousness, cleared my throat and tried again: ' – what do you suggest I do now, Comrade?'

The dark man nodded approvingly. 'That's a more sensible attitude. You'll want to go back to Eisenach now, of course. There's no reason for you to stay in Berlin any longer.'

I nodded, breathing a little more easily. Once these men let me go, and I was outside and on my own, I was sure that Nicolas or Kurt would be waiting for me. The fact that I no longer had a permit to cross to West Berlin didn't worry me in the least. Nicolas – or Kurt under Nicolas's instructions – would take care of that.

I wasn't even worried by the search that the blond man was making in the kitchen. There was nothing of mine in the apartment, nothing that didn't belong to either the real tenant or the real Elisabeth. I felt almost triumphant as he closed the kitchen cabinet and came back empty-handed to the sitting-room. There was only the bathroom left for him to search, and that contained almost nothing except for Ilse Schmidt's towels and Elisabeth's skirt and blouse and –

Oh no. *And my own underclothes with their unmistakable Marks and Spencer label, spread out on the towel rail in all their frivolously West European pink and orange flowery glory . . .*

The blond man was looking round. He took one step towards the bathroom, but I beat him to it.

'Then I must get dressed,' I cried. 'Excuse *me*, Comrade!' And I whirled inside and slammed and bolted the door in his indignant snub-nosed face.

I had never before dressed so quickly, even during backstage scene changes. The last thing I wanted was to make the men suspect that there was anything in the bathroom that I wanted to hide. My heart was hammering and my hands trembling as I pulled on my own incriminatingly brief garments, covered them with Elisabeth's shoddily serviceable clothes and flicked her comb through my hair. There was no time to bother with her hairstyle, no point in wearing her fake glasses. The men stared in surprise as I erupted into the sitting-room, fully dressed in two minutes.

'You were quick, Comrade,' approved the blond man. He gave the bathroom a cursory search, then looked me over with a gap-toothed leer. 'Some good reason for wanting to return to Eisenach, eh?'

'No doubt,' his companion agreed off-handedly. 'But first, Comrade Lorenz, I must take you to see my Chief. He would like a few words with you.'

My throat tightened. 'Your . . . Chief?'

'Just routine.'

A touch of fear made me shiver. 'But – can't I go straight back to Eisenach?'

'Just as soon as you've seen him. If you're ready, then, Comrade? Please bring all your possessions with you, there will be no need for you to return to this apartment.'

No need – or no opportunity? Was this an arrest?

My movements were slow and clumsy as I folded what I guessed were Elisabeth's things into her suitcase. This was it, then. Even if the man they were taking me to see had nothing to go on but suspicion, I could never stand up to close questioning. My German wasn't up to it, let alone my courage. My deception would be revealed within minutes, and then I should be tried and found guilty and imprisoned in East Germany for years . . .

But surely Nicolas wouldn't let it happen? He'd told Kurt to look after me – so where was Kurt?

Where above all was the man I loved?

*

The porter said nothing as I walked from the lift to the main door, a trilby-hatted man close on either side of me, but she smiled to herself as she clicked her busy needles: a Teutonic Madame Defarge, knitting away as she compiled her list of enemies of the State?

*

Another black official East German car, another drive through the streets of East Berlin. We entered another vast slab of a building, but this time it was one of the government offices on the Unter den Linden. It was quiet inside, with preoccupied people hurrying about their business. We went up several floors by lift, and then along a network of corridors. My mouth had dried so completely with fright that I began to imagine that I had lost my voice. Perhaps, I found myself hoping wildly, I shan't be able to speak a word when I'm questioned, and then they'll have to let me go!

The dark man knocked on a door and waited respectfully. A green light flashed. He went in, closing the door behind him. The blond man, who had taken charge of the suitcase, gripped my arm unnecessarily high and unnecessarily tight. Then the door opened and the dark man motioned me inside.

'This is the girl, Comrade Schildow,' he announced, and then both my escorts retreated, leaving me alone with the man behind the desk.

He was heavily built, with a short greying stubble of hair, and he stared at me through thick-lensed glasses with pale, unwinking eyes.

His voice was harsh and gravelly. 'You are Elisabeth Lorenz?' he asked, and waited for an answer.

For a moment I was tempted to tell the truth. I was

frightened and confused; since I couldn't hope to get away with it, surely the only sensible, practical thing to do was to confess and ask for leniency? If I lied to this man, my prison sentence would only be longer.

I opened my mouth, but no sound came.

The trouble was, it wouldn't just be my own punishment. The moment I blabbed I would give away everyone else. Elisabeth herself, her relatives, Kurt, even Nicolas. I should be putting them all in danger and ruining the work that Nicolas had been doing. They might even use me to get to Nicolas, releasing me but keeping me under observation so that they could arrest him the moment he came to my aid . . .

I cleared my throat, swallowed nervously and tried again. 'Yes,' I heard myself croak, 'I am Elisabeth Lorenz.'

He leaned back, still staring. 'The daughter of Doctor Udo Lorenz?'

I agreed, cautiously.

'And you have been to visit your grandmother – your maternal grandmother – in West Berlin?'

'Yes. That is so, Comrade Schildow,' I elaborated, hoping to placate him.

'Hmmm.' He got up and wandered to the window which faced a massive wall of identical windows in a parallel building. Suddenly he turned, and spoke again: 'Tell me, Comrade, when did you last see your father?'

I suppressed a hysterical desire to giggle as the painting of the Cavalier child being interrogated by Cromwellian soldiery surfaced for a second in my whirling mind. This was where the dangerously difficult part of the interview was going to begin. I tried to concentrate on the information that Nicolas had given me in his briefing.

'Er – several weeks ago,' I stammered. If he asked me for dates, I should be lost.

'And did he give you any message to give to anyone in the West?'

'There was no question of that, Comrade,' I said with

earnest ambiguity. 'His health . . .'

Schildow pulled at the fleshy lobe of his ear. 'Hmmm. Well then, who did you see while you were in the West? Who, exactly, was present in your grandmother's house?'

It must be a trap: obviously they had spies, their own sources of information. No doubt they knew exactly who lived in the house, whereas I had no idea. I tried not to flounder as I thought back frantically to the short period I had spent there, but the one person who came immediately to my mind was the one person I must not mention, Nicolas.

'I'll be glad to tell you, Comrade,' I blurted out, playing for time. I could see her strained and anxious face, but what in heaven's name was her *name*? 'My aunt – Frau Henschel!' Yes, that was it. And then there had been two other women who had bustled down from the sickroom to greet Elisabeth. 'And other relatives, of course. Two – er – cousins.'

He stared at me again, his eyes as prominent as binoculars: 'And – outsiders?' he grated. 'People who wanted to know about your father?'

'No!' I cried urgently, trying to push Nicolas's image out of my mind. 'There were no outsiders, it was just the family.'

'And what did *they* ask about your father?'

I frabricated wildly. 'About his health, of course! Naturally they were very concerned.'

'And did they give you messages to take to him?'

'No! I mean – I mean yes, of course, they sent their love and good wishes. Nothing else. Believe me, Comrade, there was so little time –'

'Hmm.' Schildow worked again on the lobe of his ear, and I was sure that he must be able to hear my heart thud in the silence of the room. Then he said, in a voice that was a little weary, almost gentle: 'Open your handbag, please, Comrade.'

'My handbag?'

'Yes.' He lifted some of his documents into a pile so

that there was a clear space before him on top of the desk. 'Empty it here, please.'

A catalogue of its contents flashed through my mind as I fumbled with the zip. Elisabeth's identity card, that was what would betray me! Had the officer at the check-point in the Wall reported the discrepancy in the colour of our eyes?

But he hadn't seemed to notice at the time; perhaps Schildow wouldn't notice it either. Otherwise, the contents of the bag were completely innocuous. I tipped them out on the desk. Elisabeth's handkerchief, Elisabeth's money, Elisabeth's railway ticket, Elisabeth's comb, Elisabeth's lipstick –

Oh no . . .

Not only Elizabeth's.

There on the desk, glittering in its gold-coloured casing, as alien among Elisabeth's drab possessions as a kingfisher at a sparrows' house party, lay my own unmistakably English lipstick.

CHAPTER 13

Schildow pounced.

'This, Comrade?' he asked, holding it up in surprisingly delicate fingers.

I moistened my lips with my tongue. 'A present. From one of my cousins in West Berlin.'

He peered distastefully at the brand name on the case. 'American?'

I didn't argue. He fiddled unfamiliarly with the case, pulled off the top and discovered the action. He twisted the base, and up rose a meagre blunted half-inch stub of lipstick.

Schildow raised his eyebrows sceptically. 'A present, Comrade?'

I cursed myself for my habit of economy, and even more for the folly which had led me to bring the lipstick with me. Nicolas had warned me, hadn't he? I remembered the occasion so clearly, down beside the Havel in the dusk, when I had wanted him to kiss me but had been afraid to let him: 'For God's sake,' he had said, 'when you go to East Berlin don't take *anything* of your own.'

And now Schildow was staring at me, the lipstick in his hand, waiting for an explanation; and on the desk in front of him was Elisabeth's identity card, describing her eyes as grey.

I kept my own blue eyes lowered, and ad-libbed frantically. 'It was the lipstick my cousin was using. I admired the colour so much that she insisted that I should take it. I have one of my own, of course – here, Comrade.'

I snatched up Elisabeth's plastic-cased lipstick and offered it to him as proof of my innocence. It was only when he started to unscrew it that I remembered with horror that it was new and completely unused.

Schildow raised his bushy eyebrows above the heavy frame of his glasses, looking from one lipstick to the other. 'So? You did not wear any of your own lip colour when you went to the West?'

'Er – no,' I babbled, 'no, as a matter of fact I didn't.' I could feel the nervous tension breaking out damply on my forehead, and I prayed that he wouldn't notice. 'I was visiting my dying grandmother, remember . . . it was out of respect for her . . .'

He nodded with apparent understanding. 'Just so, Comrade, just so. I appreciate your sensibilities. I do find it a little strange, though, that in such a short visit to your dying grandmother you still found the time and the interest to discuss lip colour with your cousin . . . ?'

I fell silent. There was nothing more I dared say. My ingenuous attempts to lie my way out of trouble had only served to get me in deeper and deeper.

Schildow was smiling grimly to himself. He turned Elisabeth's bag inside out, ripping the flimsy lining, and having satisfied himself that it contained nothing more, threw it aside and picked up my lipstick again. I watched with uneasy disbelief as he took a penknife from his pocket, scooped out the remains of the lipstick, smeared it messily and impatiently on a sheet of paper, and then began to force the case apart as though looking for a hidden note.

A knock came on the inner door. The head of a younger man, with a high-domed forehead and a neat moustache, made a deferential appearance. 'Excuse me, Comrade Schildow – '

'What is it?' Schildow growled. 'Can't you see I'm busy?'

'I'm sorry, Comrade, but this really is urgent. I've

just had a report that the Schönhausen trouble has blown up again –'

Schildow swore and threw down my lipstick and his knife. He pressed a button on his desk and my blond escort came in from the corridor.

'Put Comrade Lorenz in a room by herself until I am free again, Ullstein,' Schildow ordered. He pushed himself up heavily from his desk, then caught sight of some smears of lipstick on his hands and transferred them angrily to his handkerchief. 'That'll take some explaining to his wife,' I thought with bleak satisfaction, but Schildow had the last word.

He smiled at me without any warmth. 'I may be occupied for some little while, Comrade, but I suggest that you can usefully spend the time by reconsidering the information you have given me. It will be so much easier for you if you agree to co-operate. So, I shall look forward to continuing our conversation later.'

He jerked his head dismissively at Ullstein, who made a grab for my upper arm and marched me out of the room. I tried to pull my arm away, but his only reaction was to hold me more tightly as he pushed me ahead of him down the long corridor. I had to bite my lower lip hard to prevent myself from crying out and giving him the satisfaction of knowing how much he was hurting me.

We met one or two people in the corridor, but they all seemed to avert their eyes and melt away at our approach. All except one big man who came steadily on to meet us. My eyes were so filmed with tears of pain that I couldn't at first see him clearly, but there seemed to be something familiar about him.

I blinked. My vision cleared. 'Ku – Comrade Braun!' I cried.

He looked at me, his eyes dark and cold, and for a terrifyingly long moment I thought that his friendship had been false. He turned his head to Ullstein. 'Has Comrade Schildow finished with this girl?' he demanded.

'Hardly begun, I should say,' Ullstein replied with sadistic pleasure, but he relaxed his grip a little. 'Something else has cropped up, though, so I'm taking her to cool off until he can question her again.'

Kurt nodded, his lips compressed with anger. Then, 'You little fool,' he snarled at me. 'I do my best to help you, thinking that you're a genuine compassionate case, and then you go carrying messages to the West and getting yourself into trouble like this!'

I hung my head to prevent Ullstein from seeing the relief on my face. Of course, Kurt was having to act his way through this situation too, and making a very convincing job of it. I listened with increasing hope as he bargained, outwardly casual, with Ullstein.

'You can put her in that empty office next to mine, if you like.'

'I was going to take her down to the detention rooms.'

'Why bother to go all that way? I know there's a key to that office, it's in the door.'

Ullstein frowned. 'The window isn't barred.'

'My dear man!' Kurt scoffed. 'We're on the tenth floor – she's hardly likely to escape that way!'

'It wasn't escape I was thinking of.'

I felt a sudden rush of nausea. Dear heaven, was my situation so bad that he seriously expected me to consider jumping to my death in preference to submitting to further questions?

Kurt spoke a little less harshly. 'I don't think we need worry about that. Come on, then.'

He led the way down one corridor and into another, and opened the door of a small bare room. As he motioned me inside, I tried to resume my part and restore my credibility.

'But Comrade Braun, please can't you help me? They say my grandmother is dead and I am not allowed to go to the West today. And now they are questioning me about messages, but I took none and I certainly didn't bring any back!'

He shrugged, officially pompous. 'Comrade Schildow may, of course, find that there are no grounds for his suspicion.'

Ullstein gave a nasty laugh. 'That's what you hope, Braun! You were her escort over to the West, and you'll be in dead trouble if he does find any proof that she was carrying information about her father. I wouldn't like to be in your shoes then! Oh, and I'll keep the key to this room, thank you – she's my responsibility now.'

He slammed and locked the door, and their voices receded. I slid down the wall to a sitting position and rested my head on my knees. I was shivering, despite the growing warmth of the day. All the euphoria I had felt at the sight of Kurt had evaporated. A lot of good it would do me to be locked in the room next to his if the blond man insisted on holding the key!

Well, I was done for now. Schildow had at first been so obsessed with the idea that Elisabeth was passing information between her father and the West that he hadn't stopped to consider the fact that I might not be Elisabeth at all. But he would come to it, there was no doubt about that.

Sooner or later, he would discover that the switch had been made. And I was fairly certain, now, that I knew *why* it had been made. Elisabeth must have been carrying information of some kind that was too complicated to be passed on in a brief twenty-minute visit. That was why Nicolas had wanted her to stay for longer and why the switch was necessary.

So Schildow wasn't really barking up the wrong tree. His suspicions about Elisabeth were probably correct.

But Elisabeth herself was safe. She was down on the other side of the Wall. I was the one who was stuck up the tree, with no access to the Wall and with Ullstein guarding me until Schildow returned.

And it was Nicolas who was responsible for putting me here...

I gave way to the only luxury the room offered: the

opportunity to abandon myself to despair in complete privacy.

*

Almost immediately, it seemed, I heard the key turn in the lock.

I started up in alarm. Was Schildow ready for me so soon? Oh God, I wasn't prepared for questioning yet!

Or – almost worse – was it Ullstein coming back for a little private amusement? There was one object in the room, a broken chair and I seized and lifted it, ready to defend myself against him.

The door opened quietly. Kurt Braun slipped into the room, his finger to his lips.

I put the chair down. 'Kurt – ' I stammered. 'But how . . . ?'

He smiled. The feigned coldness and anger had gone from his eyes; they were warm and friendly. 'You didn't really imagine that I'd desert you, did you? I had a second key . . . Come on now, let's get you out of here.'

He motioned me to silence and held the door slightly ajar, listening. Then he seized my hand and pulled me into the corridor, paused to re-lock the door and pocket the key, and then ran with me towards a pair of fire doors and on to a concrete stairway.

I didn't need to be told to hurry, but anxiety made me stumble on the stairs. Kurt put a steadying arm round me and guided me down and round and down and dizzy-ingly round and seven more floors down to ground level, and at least partial freedom.

He had a car parked close to the stairway doors at the back of the building, an East German Wartburg.

'Bless you, Kurt,' I said fervently, looking back at the grim building as he accelerated away. 'I was absolutely terrified – Schildow was just on the point of finding out that I'm not Elisabeth, but then he was called away. And it was a marvellous coincidence that you appeared just as Ullstein was going to lock me up!'

He looked half-amused, half-hurt. 'Hardly a coincidence,' he protested. 'As soon as I got the message this morning that I wasn't to take you to the West, I made it my business to find out what was going on. Then I created a sizeable diversion to keep Schildow busy, and then I made a point of being in the right place at the right time.'

'For which I'm more grateful than I can say. But Kurt – what *is* going on? Is Elisabeth's grandmother really dead?'

'I have no reason to think so. No, I'm sure it was just an excuse to pick Elisabeth up. The point is that they're still convinced that you *are* Elisabeth, and that means that you've put up a wonderful perfomance. I could hardly believe that they hadn't caught you out already – if they had, they would have been on to me too. I'm deeply indebted to you for your courage.'

I shuddered. 'Don't! I've been so near to discovery so many times – I don't think I could have kept up the story a moment longer.'

'What worries me, though,' he said, frowning, 'is that *someone* must have tipped them off that Elisabeth might be carrying messages from or to her father. There must have been a deliberate leak of some kind, because no one has ever had anything against Elisabeth herself. She would never have been granted the permit to cross to the West if anyone had any doubts about her. In fact, she was such a loyal member of the East German Communist Party that she left home a couple of years ago because her father objected to her political activities. So why, suddenly, do they pick her up and suggest that she's carrying messages for him?'

'And is she,' I asked.

He shook his head, refusing to discuss the matter. 'What do you know about Elisabeth's father?' he parried.

'Very little. Nicolas told me that her father is a doctor and that he's been in a mental hospital for over a year. He said that there had been some kind of family row before her father's illness, but that Elisabeth had visited him a couple of times in hospital. In the circumstances, I wouldn't have thought that the East German government would worry about any messages he might want to send to anyone.'

'Exactly,' said Kurt impatiently. 'So why should anyone want to stir things? I could have sworn that this whole operation was watertight, but someone, somewhere, has not only ruined it but put you at a terrible risk. And I'm determined to find out who it was, though that will be difficult – I was the only person who knew about it on this side.'

I turned in my seat to stare at him. 'You mean – someone in the *West* tipped them off?'

I thought rapidly. Nicolas's boss would know about the operation, of course, but it seemed unlikely that he would betray it. Then there was George, who had been so bashful about the East German undies he had bought for me, and by now – I glanced at Elisabeth's watch and saw that it was nearly noon – would surely have raised an alarm because I hadn't come through from Elisabeth's grandmother's house into his cellar. No, I refused to believe that it could be George.

'That's impossible,' I said flatly.

'Is it?'

I folded my arms around my body, trying to suppress a shiver. 'Does Nicolas know yet that I was picked up?' I asked.

Kurt shrugged. 'I don't know what Allen knows. I don't even know where he is. I sent a message through to my contacts in the West immediately I heard you'd been picked up, asking them to tell him to get in touch with me. But I heard nothing from him before we left.'

Desolation touched my heart with a cold finger. Without consciously formulating the thought, I had taken it for granted that Kurt would be driving to a rendezvous with Nicolas. I knew that once I was with Nicolas, whichever side of the Wall we were on, everything would be all right.

But if Kurt didn't even know where Nicolas was . . .

'I think,' I said hesitantly, 'that he may be here, in East Berlin.'

Kurt stopped the car. 'Do you know exactly where?' he demanded. 'This is no time for worrying about security, my dear – if you know where he is, for goodness sake tell me and I'll take you there.'

'I only wish I knew! All I'm certain of is that he said he wouldn't be able to meet me when I got back to Elisabeth's grandmother's house, because he had some business somewhere else. I'm just guessing that it was in East Berlin.'

Kurt sighed, pushed the engine into gear and accelerated away. 'Where are we going, then?' I faltered.

'That's the problem,' he said grimly. 'You have no hope of getting through the Wall without a permit, so the best thing I can do is to get you out of Berlin and into the East German countryside. There's a popular tourist area in the Harz Mountains where you'll never be noticed among the other visitors. It's not far from the border with West Germany, and it may be possible to smuggle you across somehow. Anyway, it's the best plan I can think of for the moment. Now that you've escaped from State custody, you can't stay in East Berlin, that's for sure.'

'The Harz?' I tried to conjure up an image of the map of Germany, uncertainly locating the region to the west of Berlin. 'But – it must be at least a hundred miles away!'

'Yes, I can't possibly take you there. I must get back to my office as soon as possible, ready to deny all knowledge of your disappearance. Ah, that reminds me – '

We had been driving for some yards along the tree-lined embankment of a narrow river. Now Kurt fumbled in his pocket, drew out a key and tossed it through the open window of the car. It twisted in the air, glittering in the sunlight, before falling with a plop into the thick green water.

'There,' he said with satisfaction. 'No one knew I had it, and now that spare key's at the bottom of the Spree. As I was saying, I can't take you to the Harz myself, but I know someone who probably will. And once you're there, you must please wait in patience until help arrives. It may be several days, I'm afraid.'

Several days

If only I could discuss it with Nicolas! I hated the idea of lingering in another part of East Germany without his knowledge and approval.

'You will go on trying to contact Nicolas, won't you?' I begged. 'You'll tell him where I am and what I'm doing, so that he can come and fetch me?'

'Of course. But if I can't reach him, I'll come myself. Please don't worry. I promised to look after you, remember?'

I tried to suppress my qualms. Kurt had already proved himself a magnificently trustworthy friend, even to the extent of risking his own job.

And more than his job.

Heaven and earth, how much more selfish could I get! Kurt was an East German government official, secretly working for the West. If Schildow suspected Elisabeth, as he did, then Kurt himself must be under grave suspicion. They'd be bound to accuse him of duplicity in my escape.

And yet, not content with releasing me from detention, he was planning to go to endless trouble to get me safely over the border into West Germany. I hated to think what punishment they would hand out to him if he were caught – and yet here I was, complaining because he had no magic carpet to whirl me to freedom!

'But Kurt,' I cried impulsively, 'what about you? How will you ever talk your way out of this? Will you be all right?'

His mouth twisted in a wry smile. 'Oh, I shall just take things as they come. In my profession, danger is an occupational hazard.'

Yours – and Nicolas's too, I thought wretchedly.

The car slowed, then stopped at traffic lights. We had crossed the river. To our right, about three hundred yards away across a wasteland that had been cleared of buildings, snaked the grim grey line of the Wall. Patrols of armed border guards were thick on the ground here and I flinched as one of them stared for a moment at our stationary car.

Considering that I now had no identity card, and that as soon as my disappearance from the locked room was discovered I should be urgently wanted by the Volkspolizei, the East German police, I felt alarmingly well-qualified for honorary membership of that same dangerous profession.

CHAPTER 14

The Wall had jinxed back out of sight, we had left the armed guards behind us in the border zone, the river had become a lake. Ahead lay a park, and over the tops of some of even the tallest trees I could see the head and shoulders of a massive statue.

'The Soviet War Memorial,' said Kurt. 'It's one of the big showpieces of East Berlin, and a lot of foreign visitors go there. That's why we're going.'

He drew up in a large car park which was already half-filled with tourist coaches. Some of them were sight-seeing double-decker buses from West Berlin and I looked at them longingly.

'It's no use, my dear,' Kurt said with firm patience. 'Everyone on board has a special pass for the journey through the checkpoint – you might as well give yourself up to the nearest Vopo as try to hitch a lift in one of those. But one of the West German coach drivers is a contact of mine – ah, there he is. Wait here, please. They're used to visitors so no one will bother you.'

I sat in the car while Kurt went to talk to a roly-poly man who was leaning in the sun against the front of his coach, chewing a sandwich. There were no grey-uniformed Vopos in evidence at all, but a number of Russian soldiers in peaked caps, green tunics and breeches and knee-length boots.

I hunched down in my seat and watched with gnawing anxiety as Kurt negotiated with the coach driver. He was trying to appear casual. Although I knew that he needed urgently to get back to his office, he returned to the car at a stroll. Only his voice betrayed his relief.

'Yes, he'll do it! I can't introduce you because we don't want to make ourselves conspicuous, but his name is Willy Hendricks, and he speaks English. I've told him your real name and explained that you're holidaying in East Germany with a friend, but that you've become separated and your friend has all your luggage and documents. Willy has some spare seats and he's agreed to take you as far as Marberg, a town in the Harz. He can't possibly take you across the border, but I've told him that Marberg was the next stop on your tour and that your friend will be meeting you there. That's where I'll come for you, if I can't get in touch with Allen.'

'That's fine . . . The only thing is,' I added hesitantly, 'I haven't any money for the fare, you know.'

'Don't worry, I've arranged all that.' Kurt checked his watch, frowning. 'Now listen carefully, because I haven't much time. The coach is on one of its regular sight-seeing round trips from Hanover. The tourists have had a few days in West Berlin, and now they're off to Marberg. There's a folk festival going on there this week, that's why it's an ideal place for you to wait – it'll be crowded with visitors and you won't be noticed. The only problem is going to be accommodation.'

'Everywhere is full, I suppose?'

He shook his head impatiently. 'That's not the point. Things are done differently, here in East Germany. All tourist accommodation is State-controlled, and foreign visitors can come into East Germany only if they have booked their rooms in advance. When they come to the frontier, they are issued with visas in exchange for their hotel reservation vouchers. No accommodation, no visas. No visas, no entry.'

I pulled a wry face. 'You don't need to remind me that I'm here illegally! What do I do, then, Kurt?'

'With luck,' he explained cautiously, 'you may be able to stay at the official tourist camping site in Marberg. There's a party of young Americans travelling on the coach, on a camping tour of Europe. They have to get their camping vouchers in advance, too, but if you can manage to give the impression that you're one of their party, there's no reason why any official should suspect that you aren't a genuine tourist. The camp site will have none of the reception desk problems that you'd meet in a hotel. If you can make friends with the Americans, telling them the same story that I told the driver, I'm sure they'll be glad to help by making room for you in one of their tents.'

I could see no foundation, for his confidence. 'Oh, but that's expecting a bit much!' I protested. 'I couldn't possibly go and foist myself on them.'

He pushed his greying hair wearily off his forehead. 'There's no alternative, my dear. You can't go it alone in East Germany. If you're picked up by the Vopos you'll be finished.'

'But – supposing the Americans don't agree to help?'

He hesitated. 'In that case, you will have to ask Willy Hendricks for help,' he said reluctantly. 'He has relatives in the town, but for that reason he has to be doubly careful. I'd rather not involve him any further, so please go to him only as a last resort. Oh, don't worry.' Kurt smiled at me reassuringly. 'I'm quite sure the Americans will appreciate your problem and be glad to help. You'll be all right. Just stay with them, so that I know where to find you – I won't let you down, I promise. But I really must go now or the Vopos will be out looking for both of us.'

I pulled myself together. I was being selfish again. Kurt was taking a terrible risk to help me, and I was wasting his time over foolish objections.

'I'm sorry,' I apologised, scrambling out of the car. 'I'll do as you say, of course. Only – you will try to let Nicolas know where I am, won't you?'

He sighed, but nodded his acknowledgement.

Poor Kurt. It was tactless of me to remind him so frequently of my emotional dependence on Nicolas. Nicolas, who had got me into this mess, wasn't here to get me out of it. For my present safety, and therefore my future happiness, I was utterly dependent on Kurt. The least I could do was to show him my gratitude.

Impulsively, I put my hand through the open window of his car. He hesitated for a moment, then took it eagerly.

I smiled at him. 'Thank you,' I said, 'from the bottom of my heart.'

He looked at me for a moment, intent, unsmiling, then lifted my hand briefly to his lips. I stood watching as he drove quickly out of sight, and then I turned and walked towards the West German coach.

*

The tubby driver had finished his sandwich and was now enjoying a pipeful of tobacco in the warmth of the sun.

'Good morning, Herr Hendricks,' I said. It was a relief to be able to speak in English, for the first time since I had left Nicolas, and not to have to try to remember to address people as Comrade.

He nodded at me comfortably, taking the pipe from his mouth. '*Guten Tag, Fräulein.* Call me Willy, everybody does. Happy to have you with us as far as Marberg.' He looked at his watch. 'We shall leave here in ten minutes.'

He gave me another friendly nod and waddled away, his pipe sticking from his teeth at a jaunty angle, to speak to the driver of a newly-arrived tourist coach. I stood staring uneasily at the massive white colonnades and statues of the Memorial that towered above the car park, nervously conscious of my aloneness and total lack of possessions. Would anyone believe the story Kurt had invented for me?

About a dozen men and girls, most of them rather younger than I was, were heading back towards the coach. Several of them had the name of an American university blazoned across their tee-shirts. They looked a very pleasant, friendly crowd, but even so I didn't relish the prospect of proposing myself as a member.

I moved away from the door of the coach, wretchedly uncertain of my next move, and then, totally unexpectedly, it was made for me.

'Monumental sort of place, isn't it?' said a gloomy young American voice at my elbow.

I turned eagerly. He was about my own height, and a good deal younger than the others in the group; probably fifteen or sixteen years old, very slim, but with disproportionately long legs and wide shoulders that suggested that he still had a good deal of growing to do. His voice was deep, but his cheeks still boyishly rounded. He looked, I thought, with his engagingly upturned nose and his fair hair curling round his ears and on to his forehead, extraordinarily like a Botticelli angel in jeans.

And like an angel, he had appeared at a most propitious time. I seized the opening he offered.

'Monumental was exactly the word I wanted,' I agreed.

He looked at me with interest, his head on one side. 'You're English, aren't you? My name's Scott Fletcher. Hey, how come I haven't seen you on the coach before? I mean, I couldn't not have *noticed* you. Have you just joined, or something? Are you on your own?'

I drew a deep breath and told him the story that Kurt had given me. 'It's just a matter of somewhere to stay while I'm waiting, you see,' I finished. 'There'll be endless bother if I arrive at the tourist hotel in Marberg without any papers.'

'Don't even think of trying it,' Scott warned. 'The hassle there was at the checkpoint when we tried to cross the Wall into East Berlin, just because I'd lost my camping voucher! How was I to know it was so important?'

'Wouldn't the East Germans let you through?'

He shook his head. 'Uh-uh. It took us a whole day out of the trip, just to get my papers sorted. Now we've missed visiting the Sans-Souci Palace at Potsdam, and my sister Nancy is so mad at me that she'll hardly speak.' He pushed the curls out of his eyes with a rather grubby hand. 'I guess I am a little young for them, at that,' he observed wistfully. 'The others are all in pairs – it gets kind of lonely.'

I knew exactly how he felt. 'Yes,' I agreed, and there was nothing artificial about the desolation in my voice.

He studied me, charmingly diffident. 'Look, I don't want to seem pushy,' he said earnestly, 'but if you're coming on your own as far as Marberg, maybe you could team up with us?'

I accepted with alacrity. 'I'd be most grateful, Scott,' I said equally seriously. 'As long as your sister and her friends agree, of course.'

The boy beamed. 'Why shouldn't they?' he demanded, ushering me into the coach and swinging himself into the seat beside me.

I could think of several good reasons, but none that I could mention.

Scott introduced me to a bewildering succession of names and faces as the rest of the group boarded the coach, and we all said 'Hi'. Willy, the driver, manoeuvred the coach out of the park and Scott's sister Nancy and her dark, stocky friend Paul settled in the seat in front of us and turned to talk.

They were clearly ready to be friendly, until Scott blurted out the story I had told him. 'So of course,' he finished eagerly, 'I said that as Alison didn't have her visa with her, she'd better stay with us until her boy-friend arrives. She can have my tent.'

Nancy and Paul exchanged wary looks.

'You're in a tough spot,' commented Paul, sympathetic but in no rush to help.

'We know what a problem these documents can be,' agreed Nancy. 'Eh, Scott?' She looked hard at her brother. The golden-haired family likeness was unmistakable, but there was a definite chill in the air. 'If you lose your papers now,' she warned him, 'we'll never get you out of East Germany, you know that? They'll imprison you for sure.'

Scott blushed and wriggled. 'Of *course* I won't lose

them,' he muttered, 'not now I *know*. But Alison hasn't lost hers, she just needs a bit of help until her boy-friend catches up with her. Oh, come on, Nancy, how would you feel if you were in her place?'

There was a long moment of hesitation. Paul and Nancy looked at each other uncertainly, and Scott looked appealingly from one to the other like an outsize puppy who doesn't care which one makes the decision to take him for a walk, as long as the decision is made.

'If there's the least hint of bother when we get to the camp site,' I promised breathlessly, praying that it was a promise I wouldn't be called on to honour, 'I'll make it absolutely clear that you don't know me.'

Nancy shrugged, then smiled. 'That's it, then. If the East Germans let you into the camp, I guess we'll be glad to help from then on.' She nodded cordially and turned away.

'Oh, that's great!' Scott exclaimed. 'Everything'll be fine, Alison. I'll take care of you.'

I realised that my hands had been trembling with tension. Now they relaxed a little. 'Thank you so much for your help, Scott,' I said.

'You're welcome,' he replied grandly, enjoying his new rôle of protector. Then he added: 'When did you say you were expecting your boy-friend to meet you?'

'Oh . . . I'm not exactly sure . . . Within the next day or two.'

He frowned. 'He *is* coming to Marberg?'

'I hope so, Scott,' I said fervently.

Dear heaven I hoped so.

CHAPTER 15

Scott talked virtually without pause from East Berlin to the Hartz, and I was glad of it. Glad too, to be heading westwards, even though I knew that the heavily-guarded border lay between me and freedom. The fact that I was temporarily with a group of people to whom the border guards presented no threat, made me feel slightly less trapped.

The coach carried us at speed across the intensively cultivated North German plain and then, beyond Magdeburg, turned off the autobahn and headed south-west on little-used roads. The countryside became more intimate, with rolling hills and frequent villages and farmsteads. The road was dusty, but shaded in places by wild cherry trees whose ripe fruit brushed against the windows of the coach as we passed. In the fields women in long dark dresses, with white scarves protecting their heads from the sun, stopped working as we approached, straightened their backs and waved, and all of us, the driver included, waved back.

And then, with the evening sun blinding our eyes, we threaded along even narrower roads through the wooded mountains of the Harz, and came at last to Marberg.

We saw the town first from a hilltop half a mile away. I could remember, from my childhood in Thuringia, seeing a good many picturesque little German towns – but never one that came, like this, straight out of an illustrated book of fairy tales.

Marberg was set securely on the top of a steep, wooded, rocky hill, high above a river that meandered through meadows golden and pink with wild flowers. The town was compact, walled-in as a protection against medieval enemies. Above the snaking stone wall, set at intervals with red-roofed watch towers and bastioned gateways, rose a jumble of half-timbered gables, red-tiled roofs hung at crazy angles, sturdy bell towers and delicate slated spires whose gilded finials glittered as they caught the setting sun. At one end of the town, looking like an upward extension of the rock it stood on, towered the sheer walls and turrets of an imposing castle.

'Wow!' breathed Scott reverently. 'Is that for real, or am I just imagining it?'

Willy Hendricks, who acted as guide as well as driver, had stopped the coach to give us the benefit of the view. He used the stem of his pipe to point out landmarks, and gave us a potted history of the town including the storming of the castle in the sixteenth-century peasants' revolt, the subject of the festival that the tourists had come to see.

'Who lives in the castle now?' asked one of the girls. 'Is it still the same family?'

'No, no, Fräulein,' Willy explained patiently. 'This is *East* Germany. Castles like this all belong to the State. Some are left to ruin, some – like this one – are homes for the old or sick, some are museums for tourists. The East German government now wishes to encourage tourists, and that is why they allow the townspeople to hold their festival again.'

'And is that the camp site?' asked Paul, pointing. Among the trees at the foot of the hill on which the town was set, we could glimpse the blue and orange of tents.

'That is so,' Willy said, tucking his pipe away and starting his engine. 'There will be rehearsals for the festival in the town tomorrow morning,' he told us over his shoulder as he drove down the hill. 'And in the afternoon the pageant itself. And you will be ready for me to take you across the border and back to Hanover the day after, *nicht*?'

'Right,' Nancy agreed.

Two days, then . . .

I would have just two days with the Americans, and after that I should be on my own. Nowhere to stay, no money, no possessions, no visa, no passport. No friends.

What was happening to Kurt? I wondered. My escape would have been discovered hours ago. Had they suspected him immediately? Were they interrogating him now?

Had he had time to get in touch with Nicolas first?

All the others were excited as we approached the camp site, looking forward to stretching their legs and having a meal and exploring the town. Even Scott had temporarily forgotten me and, fraternal relations restored, was leaning over the seat in front to tease his sister. For a long, chilling five minutes I felt isolated: an outsider accompanying them on false pretences, an illegal entrant to the country, a woman wanted by the East Berlin Volkspolizei. I felt alarmingly vulnerable – cold, tense, queasy, utterly alone.

We had crossed the swift clear river by an old stone bridge and were now driving along a road that looped through the meadows at the foot of the hill. Above us, wooded slopes rose up towards the encircling stone wall of the town. And then we reached the point where the trees gave way to the sheer outcrop of rock on which the castle was perched, and we all craned our necks to look up through the roof lights of the coach at the massive, centuries-old walls of the stronghold towering above.

'Sure beats Disneyland,' someone said.

I could see his point. With its sheer walls, its round Rapunzel corner turrets, each with a single high oriel window and a conical cap of red tiles, and its massive steeply-pitched central roof in which rows of small windows were set under individually outcurving eaves, giving the impression of eyes peering from under eyebrows, Marberg appeared to be the original of every castle in the entire works of the Brothers Grimm.

But their famous name carried, at that moment, no happy childhood connotation. To me in my distress, Marberg Castle looked grim enough to be a prison.

*

Scott, and his sister and Paul, were as quiet and tense as I was when we approached the camp site, and we all sighed with relief when the man in charge allowed us to enter with only a cursory glance at the mass of papers Paul gave him. There was no attempt to count heads. The site was crowded, and the man had problems enough without looking for more.

The boys quickly unloaded all the gear from the coach, and Willy drove it away. The routine was obviously well-practised: Scott worked busily on his own, putting up one very small ridge tent while the others erected bright pavilions on metal frames. When he had finished, Scott beckoned me over to admire his work.

'This is mine, Alison,' he said proudly. 'I've used it since I was so high. I'd like you to consider it yours, as long as you're with us.'

I'd never slept in a tent of any kind, let alone one with a ridge. It sagged alarmingly in the middle, and I had visions of it collapsing on me in the early hours of the morning.

'Thank you very much, Scott,' I said. 'It's sweet of you, but I couldn't possibly turn you out – '

'No bother,' he said eagerly. 'I can sleep in the open – I'd like to, truly.'

Nancy had been listening and now she strolled over to join us.

'Believe it or not,' she said, 'you'll have more room there than we have in the girls' tent – it's a crush, I can tell you. It may not look like it, but Scott's is a good offer – I should take it if I were you.'

'Gladly,' I said quickly. 'I feel bad about turning your brother out, though.'

Nancy tucked a strand of long fair hair back behind her ear and gave her brother a drily affectionate look. 'Oh, I shouldn't worry about that – all this medieval scenery is making him feel chivalrous, eh, Scott? If you have any dragons you need slaying, Alison, I think he'll be glad to oblige. And if you haven't, the least you can do is to allow him to sleep in the open on your account! He'll be fine in his sleeping bag, and if you come over to our tent I'll fix you up with a blanket.'

But it was more than a blanket I needed, of course. They were all extremely kind and helpful but I felt wretchedly, embarrassingly dependent as someone found me a clean towel and others lent soap and a comb. Everyone was too polite to comment, but the fact that I had nothing at all with me, apart from what I was wearing, obviously made them uneasy.

I hated being unable to tell them more. I liked them, they had been wonderfully good to me, and I longed to be able to repay them by telling them the truth.

But the truth would hardly make them happy. To admit the true extent of my predicament would be to make them accessories to my offences against the East German State. They would, quite rightly, be frantic with worry and vicarious guilt, and I should have no alternative but to leave them immediately. So I did my best to swallow the generous supper they gave me, and tried to smile, and prayed that Nicolas would by now have heard where I was and that he would be on his way to rescue me.

I insisted on doing the lion's share of the washing-up, and no one objected, though of course Scott helped. By the time we had finished, it was growing dark. Most of the group had decided to walk up to the town and sample the local brew in a tourist inn, but although Scott eagerly offered to escort and treat me, I declined.

We sat outside the tent for a while, watching the last of the light fade from the walls of the castle high above us. Scott asked what work I did, and his interest and excitement when he heard that I was an actress was so great that I hadn't the heart to disillusion him about the profession. But I was too weary to indulge him for long.

'I think I'll turn in. But look, Scott, are you going to be all right in the open?'

'Sure. I'll be fine in my sleeping bag.' He demonstrated, kicking off his sneakers, scrunching himself down into the bag fully dressed, and embarking on a recital of long, whistling snores.

I laughed. 'All right,' I conceded, 'I'll believe you. Just don't keep *me* awake by snoring, that's all. Good night – and thank you for everything.'

Tired though I was, I was far too worried to sleep. I turned and wriggled restlessly on the unyielding ground, while my mind clamoured with problems. It wasn't until I heard Scott clear his throat, astonishingly close, that I remembered that only a wall of canvas separated us.

'Alison?' he said quietly.

'Mmm?' I feigned sleepiness, not wanting to bother with idle chat.

'This friend of yours – Nicolas. Are you going to marry him?'

I stiffened, feeling the colour rise in my cheeks and aware of the rough caress of the blanket against them. 'Good heavens, I don't know,' I mumbled. 'The question hasn't arisen.'

'Ah!' The relief in his voice was unmistakable.

'You wouldn't approve, I take it?' I said, trying to keep my voice light.

'We-ell,' he answered judiciously, 'something *is* bothering me. You say Nicolas brought you here to East Germany on vacation, and then you were separated? And he has your purse and your passport and your visa and your luggage and everything?'

I made an uncomfortable murmur of assent. It did sound a very thin story.

There was a moment's silence, and then he burst out defiantly: 'Well, if I had a girl like you, I know one thing – I sure as hell wouldn't *lose* her! I mean . . . to let himself be separated from you, and to leave you stranded in a country like this, where they'll lock you up for stepping out of line . . . how could he be so *dumb*?'

I swallowed hard. 'I don't really think – ' I began, but he cut in quickly.

'Oh, I know it's none of my business, and I don't mean to be rude or hurtful. But – well, even if you were just an ordinary *friend*, you'd think he'd take more care of you. But you're in love with him, aren't you? I could tell that whenever you mentioned him. I'm sorry, Alison, but I just don't think he's the right man for you. If he were, he'd look after you a whole lot better than this!'

I hadn't allowed myself to consider it, let alone admit it. But as I pulled the blanket over my head and pressed my fist hard against my mouth in an effort to keep my desolation from the boy, I had to acknowledge that what he said was true.

CHAPTER 16

It was a long time before I could sleep. Scott's criticism of Nicolas had been too painfully accurate. And he didn't know the half of it!

It was true. Nicolas was irresponsible, inconsiderate – and worse. He must have known full well the risks that were involved when he talked me into switching places with Elisabeth. To put me, deliberately, in such danger was not the act of a friend, let alone that of a man worth loving.

I had to face up to it. Quite probably Nicolas wouldn't come to rescue me. Even if he wasn't as irresponsible as I feared, it was possible that Kurt's message hadn't reached him. And perhaps poor Kurt himself was already under arrest for conniving at my escape from East Berlin.

Perhaps there was no one to come to my rescue at all.

And yet I couldn't rely on Paul and Nancy and their friends either. They had already done more than enough to help me. And Kurt had made it clear that I must not involve Willy Hendricks if I could avoid it. Willy was to be approached only as a last resort, so in fairness to him I must wait at least until tomorrow evening before begging for his help.

In the meantime, the important thing was not to worry my companions. I must act confidently and naturally, as though the story I had told them was true. More acting . . .

When I emerged from the tent next morning, stiff

from sleeping on the ground, Scott had disappeared. But in a few moments he was back, running, with fresh warm rolls that he had fetched from the town. He was ebullient, proud of his night spent in the open on my behalf, and eager to inform the others that I had made a stage appearance in London. I guessed that his rescue of an actress from a tight situation was going to make a good story to tell his friends when he got back home.

I watched him affectionately as we breakfasted, thinking how urgently I needed the services of a resourceful Knight Errant. He caught my eye, and gulped the last of his coffee. 'The town's really fantastic,' he announced. 'I'm going back there right away – there's so much I want to photograph. You'll come with me, won't you, Alison?'

I was glad to. Anything, to take my mind off my own problems.

The main gate of the camp site led out to a road that wound up the hill towards one of the bastioned gateways of the town. This was the route that most people from the camp were taking, but after Scott had burrowed into his tent and emerged backwards clutching his camera, he led me to a smaller gate at the far end of the site.

'I found this path when I came down from the town this morning,' he explained. 'It cuts up through the trees to a sort of back door in the town walls. It's a lot quicker and prettier than the road, but it *is* a bit steep. Sure you'll be able to manage?'

I assured him gravely that I thought I could. As he said, it was pleasant under the trees: the hot sun came filtering through the leaves, and although there was one path that went almost straight up the hill, another one nearby zig-zagged sufficiently to make it a walk rather than a scramble. Even so, I was glad when, towards the top, the ground levelled a little and the trees thinned sufficiently to allow grass to grow. I moved away from the path and sat down, my back against a convenient tree trunk, and looked out across the tops of the hillside trees to the rolling miles of sunlit countryside, shade-swept by fat white wind-chased clouds.

Scott had been chatting, tirelessly. It wouldn't be reasonable to expect a trainee Knight Errant to be perfect. Now he broke off and sniffed the air.

'What's that scent?'

I had recognised it immediately, as soon as we had climbed up through the oaks and chestnuts to this natural grassy platform. The pale yellow flowers were hanging above us in thick clusters against the tender green leaves, and their scent – honey-sweet, elusive, unforgettable – came drifting down to us.

'We're sitting under a linden tree,' I said. 'If we're quiet, we shall be able to hear the bees.'

He stopped talking for a full three minutes. I leaned my head against the trunk of the tree, and closed my eyes. The air was warm and blessedly quiet; the traffic in the valley was a distant murmur. Nearer, there was the ripple and splash of a fast-falling stream, and nearer still the absorbed humming of a thousand drunken bees among the lime flowers.

Linden, I corrected myself wretchedly. Not lime, linden.

The scent pervaded the air. 'Nicolas,' I thought in despair, 'Nicolas, my love, where are you? You can't abandon me like this, surely you can't – ?'

There was a sudden sharp click. I opened my eyes with a start. Scott, his camera to his eye, was taking some quick close-ups of me. I tossed a handful of grass at him to make him stop.

'All right, then,' he agreed, holding out a large paw and pulling me to my feet. 'Let's get up to the town before it's too crowded.'

The path wound upwards through the trees and emerged at the foot of the massive encircling town wall. A narrow dirt road, rising from another part of the valley, led on up an open slope to an archway in the wall surmounted by a red-roofed watch tower. We walked up the slope, through the archway under the tower, and then up a lane between high garden walls overhung by apple trees. And then, climbing some stone steps, we reached one of the main streets of Marberg.

As Scott had said, the town was fantastic. Truly fantastic – for once, the much misused adjective provided an exact description. Marberg looked unbelievably unreal, a town transported in its entirety from the Middle Ages to the twentieth century. I felt that I was in a fantasy-town, a story-book setting come to life.

We joined the other tourists and wandered, I gaping, Scott clicking his camera with the speed of a fashion photographer. Marberg was a town of cobbled streets lined by tall gabled houses, some of stone, but most of them half-timbered, with brown beams and plaster-work shading from cream to ochre. Dormer windows peered down at us from steeply-pitched roofs. On street corners, charmingly extravagant half-timbered circular bay windows, topped by individual turrets, projected from upper storeys.

Stone towers sprouted everywhere: church towers, bell towers, watch towers, castle towers; some round, some square, some topped with conical roofs, some with spires, some with onion domes. On top of one of the highest was perched a watchman's house, half-timbered, its tiled roof ridged and gabled in a shape reminiscent of the helmets of sixteenth-century German knights in engravings by Dürer.

But although I was enchanted by the appearance of the town, I found it impossible to forget that I was in East Germany, and no tourist. At the end of every street we caught sight of the encircling wall. Not an open-topped wall, like the ones I had walked round in York and Chester, but one with a red-tiled roof that covered the walkway. It was a delightful wall, curving and turning, its stones cushiony with lichens. In some places it had been used as the fourth side of an old house, or of a barn or poultry shed. Grass and wild flowers grew at its base, logs were stacked against it, children bounced balls off it. It had been tamed, domisticated.

But it was still a wall, and for me it was an ever-present reminder of the Wall in Berlin, and of the fact that I was on the wrong side of the East-West frontier.

'Isn't it marvellous?' cried Scott. 'Just look at the *detail* – those elaborate old wrought-iron signs over the shops and the carved corner-posts and the stone fountains with knights and heraldic creatures on the top . . .'

'And I love those geraniums cascading out of window-boxes,' I agreed, trying to shake off my worries, 'and – oh, can you hear the music?'

The insistent sound of fife and drum began to draw the crowds through the narrow streets and into an open place in front of the castle. Its massive doors were firmly closed, but the sightseers were expectant. Apparently the festival pageant was being rehearsed, and the castle doors would soon be opened.

The musicians and, it seemed, half the townspeople, were already dressed for the festival. Some were wearing the old regional costume, the men in wide-brimmed hats, black velvet waistcoats and knee-breeches, the women in full-length gathered skirts with ornately-embroidered bodices, and pleated white bonnets. Others had made a cheerful stab at dressing for the period of the pageant, give or take a century.

'Will you look at him,' hooted Scott, pointing to a portly burgher dressed in a plumed hat, seventeenth-century jerkin and thigh boots. 'He's a hundred years too late for the Peasants' Revolt!'

'Oh, but see how he's enjoying himself! Dressing-up's such fun. Besides, I imagine they're wearing whatever they can unearth from their lumber rooms. Look, some of the men are just wearing hats and cloaks over their ordinary clothes, but does it matter? They're all entering into the spirit of the thing.'

A group of costumed men approached the castle doors, leading a waggon drawn by a pair of heavy-shouldered, cream-coloured oxen. Two armed members of the Volkspolizei who had been standing guard drew aside. The great doors were dragged open from the inside, and a muffled cheer went up from the crowd as the waggon lumbered under the stone gateway and into the castle courtyard.

From the comments of the crowd, I gathered that it was rare for anyone from the town to enter the castle. I craned my neck in an attempt to see inside, but glimpsed only the bare courtyard and a solid wall, relieved by rows of small windows; a bleak place to be used as a home for the old and sick. I couldn't be sure, but I thought I could see pale faces staring down into the courtyard from some of the windows.

And then the oxen came out again, and a greater cheer went up as the waggon rolled into view with an enormous cask aboard. According to the story Willy had told us, a tyrannical sixteenth-century Duke had agreed to spare the lives of the rebellious peasantry only if ten of the citizens could, between sunrise and sunset on one summer day, drink every drop of wine in the biggest cask in his castle cellars. If this was the original cask, I thought, then the ten citizens would have been paralytic before they'd drunk a fraction of it, and been hanged into the bargain.

'Bet the cask's empty,' muttered Scott cynically, but the thought didn't take the smile of enjoyment from his face; or rather from what I could see of his face since his camera had become a permanent feature in front of his eye, endlessly clicking.

A procession formed, directed by a perspiring man in *lederhosen* that were dark and shiny with years of wear. The fife and drum band took its place in front of the patient-eyed indifferent oxen, and began banging and shrilling its way towards the market place. As the waggon rumbled over the cobblestones, anyone with any pretensions to costume – and a good many local children and dogs without – fell in behind. And then, since there was nothing more to watch, the spectators followed too.

Scott moved to another viewpoint. I stayed to watch as the oxen and waggon approached the place where I was standing, interested and amused despite my worries.

And then I saw Nicolas.

It was impossible, of course. If Nicolas were here, in Marberg, he wouldn't be walking in procession at a rehearsal for a pageant, wearing a broad-brimmed black hat and a short jaunty cloak slung over one shoulder.

Impossible.

And yet . . .

The man was past before I had begun to gather my wits. I tried to push my way through the crowds, but found myself caught up in the tail end of the procession. I struggled free, elbowing my way rudely through the onlookers until I reached the open space behind them, and then running full pelt until I was level with the head of the procession again.

'Alison!'

It was Scott, grabbing my arm as I flew past. 'Alison, what's going on?'

'It's Nicolas,' I gasped. 'I'm sure I've just seen Nicolas!'

The boy looked half-pleased, half-sorry. 'Hasn't he seen you yet?'

'No. You carry on with your photographs, Scott, while I find him. I'll see you back at the camp.'

He let go of my arm reluctantly. 'Don't get lost, now.'

I flashed a smile at the boy and dodged away until I was level with the oxen again, then pushed my way through to the front row of spectators. The waggon rolled past. Behind it were girls and men in regional costume, a jester in parti-coloured hose, the fat man in the buff jerkin, a girl in a dirndl dress and print head-scarf. I stood on my toes, bobbing frantically in an effort to see if he had moved to the other side of the group.

And then I saw him. He was wearing an ordinary shirt and trousers under his short cloak, narrow trousers which I was sure were part of Nicolas's suit. I recognised his walk. His face was partly shadowed by the hat he wore, but I recognised the turn of his head. Even if you have known him only a short time, the simplest movements of the man you love are unmistakable.

He was within a few yards of me, and all my questions, my doubts, my worries about his good faith, my unhappiness, were blotted out by the fact of his presence.

'Nicolas!' I called, hearing my voice break with joy and relief. 'Nicolas, here I am!'

He walked on, looking straight ahead, hardly a muscle of his face moving.

My heart seemed to stop. I stood still, buffeted by the people pushing past me, staring after him. Was it a mistake? Was this man Nicolas's double, as I was Elisabeth's?

But that would be far too great a coincidence. And anyway, as I knew, even people who look alike don't walk in the same way. This *was* Nicolas, I was positive. Perhaps he hadn't heard me above the noise of the band.

I shoved and scrambled after him, and caught at his arm. For a second he paused. I looked up at him and saw the familiar long-lashed green-brown eyes; saw too the small unmistakably identifying scar on his cheek.

'Nicolas,' I said simply.

My hand instinctively moved up and on to his shoulder. I raised my face, I waited for his kiss.

He looked straight at me without any sign of recognition. He shook off my hand. He side-stepped. He brushed past me and walked on.

CHAPTER 17

I was lost. Caught up in the crowds like a stick tossed into a flowing stream and swept and jostled along without volition or purpose. I couldn't distinguish Nicolas, somewhere ahead of me among the costumed townspeople, because my vision was blurred.

Eventually I found myself beached on the steps of the town hall. In front of me, the market place was awash with excitement. The wine cask was being set up in the centre, the fifes and drums were in competition with a silver band, the hot and bothered master of ceremonies was trying to separate those who were taking part in the rehearsal from the onlookers.

I no longer had any idea where among the crowds Nicolas might be. All I knew for certain was that he was here in Marberg, and that far from having come to rescue me, he refused even to acknowledge my existence. Scott had been right: even an ordinary friend would have taken more care of me.

But perhaps Nicolas had been too preoccupied with something else to talk to me at that moment? I tried to think of excuses for him, of possible reasons for his blank stare. Perhaps he had been injured in some way and lost his memory? Perhaps I ought to find him and try to help him?

But the recollection of the brusque way he had shaken off my hand and pushed past me was a humiliating deterrent. If he hadn't been prepared to recognise me then, he would not now. Nothing would induce me to seek another rebuff.

Besides it was ludicrous to imagine that, with my problems, I could be of help to anyone.

And yet I couldn't tear myself away. If Nicolas was here, in the market place, I wanted to be near him. He might not want my help but I certainly needed his.

The clock on the town hall struck twelve and the clocks from the town's other towers echoed and answered. The rehearsal for the pageant seemed to be over. The bandsmen saved their breath for the afternoon, the main participants began to disperse, the wine cask was heaved back on the waggon and the oxen pulled it away. The market place began to empty of everyone except tourists.

I lingered, standing full in the sunlight on top of the town hall steps. If Nicolas wanted to find me, he would have no difficulty.

*

Apparently he didn't want to find me.

I stood there, desolate, until it seemed that a Vopo was beginning to take too much notice of me. Then, heartsick, I stumbled away.

I had no idea where to find the path Scott and I had come up, but I recognised some of the American group and followed them, keeping at a distance. The last thing I wanted was company. My one idea was to get back to the privacy of the tent and it seemed that the Americans were returning to the camp. They took the main gate out of the town, followed the road down the hill and turned off along the lane that led to the site. I trailed after them, so numbed and dazed that at first I hardly noticed the man who was standing just outside the camp entrance.

As soon as he saw me, he stepped forward. Once again Kurt Braun had come to my rescue.

There was no hesitation in his manner now, no trace of the original shyness. His face was weary, as though he had had very little sleep, but the tiredness seemed to lift with his smile of recognition and welcome.

'I've come, my dear,' he said, holding out both his hands.

Relief and gratitude overwhelmed me. In that moment I saw that Kurt, with his greying hair and broad shoulders, represented exactly what I needed: help, stability, security. I clung to his outstretched hands as if they were a lifebelt.

His look changed to one of anxiety. 'Why – what's the matter? You look as though you had seen a ghost.'

He put a reassuring arm around me and led me to a bench beside the path, and for the moment I allowed myself the luxury of leaning on his shoulder. I felt limp with relief that at least my most urgent practical problem had been solved.

Kurt had proved a magnificent friend. Now that he was here, I need have no more worries about getting out of East Germany. I was vaguely aware, as I sat in his comforting embrace that Scott Fletcher came past, saw us, hesitated and walked on; but my other problems were too great to allow me to acknowledge the boy just then, let alone involve myself in introductions.

I pulled myself together and sat up. Kurt released me reluctantly, watching me with concern as he waited for my answer.

'Thank goodness you've come, Kurt,' I said shakily, pushing my hair back from my face. 'I've been absolutely desperate for the past hour. Nicolas is here, in the town – I've seen him and touched him and spoken to him, but he just looked straight through me. I don't understand!'

Kurt frowned. 'Here in Marberg? Are you absolutely sure? But I wasn't able to get a message to him. That's why I came to help you myself. He couldn't possibly know you were here – you must be mistaken.'

I shook my head. 'I couldn't be sure, at first. He was in a procession and wearing a hat that partly hid his face. But I went up close to him as close as I am to you, and I *know* it was him! After all, I love him. You can't mistake a man you love.'

There was hurt in his eyes, but his voice was gentle and understanding. 'No,' he said, 'I'm sure you can't. And this is what makes the situation so very much worse for you. It means, you see, that my suspicions were right.' He took my unresisting hands in his. 'My dear, I am very sorry.'

'Sorry for what?' I asked him blankly. 'What suspicions are you talking about?'

He tightened his grasp and answered slowly and quietly: 'About your friend Nicolas Allen.'

My mind was like a paperweight that had been shaken up to produce a snowstorm; everything whirled and eddied.

'I – I don't know what you mean,' I stammered, pulling my hands away.

He let out a long breath. 'I mean . . . I hate to have to tell you this, but I mean that I think that Allen has tricked you. He has used you and then betrayed you.'

I stared at him, horrified. 'No!' I cried. 'How dare you say that. It's not true, it can't possibly be true . . .'

But even as I said it, a cold sick feeling in the pit of my stomach told me that I was protesting too much.

Kurt slid his arm along the back of the bench and rested his hand lightly and affectionately on my shoulder. 'It's hard for you to accept this, I know. But if we were in the West and you were the girl I loved –' he hesitated for a moment, then went on, ' – I would never dream of allowing you to go to East Germany illegally. The risk is too great. No one who really loved you would ask you to do it.'

I bowed my head. I'd heard it all before, from Scott. I knew that it was true.

'And then,' Kurt went on, with soft-spoken but remorseless logic, 'there is the mystery of why you were picked up in East Berlin. You played your part admirably – no one suspected that you were not the real Elisabeth. And no one mistrusted the real Elisabeth, or she would never have been given a permit to go to the West. Someone betrayed her – but betrayed her when she was safely on the other side. Someone wanted her to be kept over there, and was prepared to sacrifice you in order to do it.'

I moved away from him, feeling my cheeks redden with angry incredulity. 'But Nicolas would never have . . .'

Kurt raised a sceptical eyebrow. 'No? My dear, he is an intelligence agent. He is clever, good at his job, dedicated to his career. But it's not a career that allows room for emotional entanglements – I know that to my own cost. An agent always has to put his work first. If Allen has told you that he loves you, it *may* be true. On the other hand, you have to face the fact that he may simply have been talking of love in order to persuade you to help him.'

I jumped to my feet, oblivious of the inquisitive stares of some campers walking along the path to the site. 'It's not true,' I protested loudly. 'He never mentioned love.' But I was trembling. I remembered the reason for my reluctance to let Nicolas kiss me. Kurt was merely confirming what I had suspected then, beside the Havel.

Kurt rose and stood behind me. 'I'm sorry that I had to tell you this so brutally,' he said. 'I had hoped that you might have come to see it for yourself. I'm afraid that the word of an agent simply can't be trusted – it's what he does to help you that counts, and Allen hasn't been very helpful, has he?'

I gave a choking laugh. That was the understatement of the year. Not only had Nicolas got me into this mess but just now, when he saw me alone and bewildered in an East German town, he had not so much as twitched a muscle in recognition, let alone made any attempt to help me.

I turned to Kurt. The snow scene in my mind had begun to whirl again. 'But at least he's here,' I insisted, trying to give myself hope. 'That must mean *something.*'

Kurt shrugged. 'Oh, he has business of his own here, no doubt. I don't know what it is, but I'm afraid that you must accept the fact that he didn't come to rescue you. He was taking part in the festival, did you say?'

'Yes – wearing a hat and a cloak.'

We both looked uncomprehendingly up the hill towards the walled town. Immediately above us the castle rose sheer from the rock, its turrets jousting at the scurrying white clouds.

'I don't understand it,' Kurt said heavily. 'I can't imagine what he's doing.' Then he looked at me, his face grim with anger. 'But by God, I'd like to know! I'd like to find him and have it out with him! How *dare* he make such cold, callous use of you. When I think of the danger you were in, in East Berlin . . . Thank God I was able to get you out of that!'

The thought of my hideous predicament in East Berlin made me weak at the knees. I sat down again on the bench. What was it Kurt had said? 'The word of an agent can't be trusted, it's what he does to help that counts . . .'

Well, there could be no doubt about Kurt's trustworthiness. He had helped me to escape, first from custody and then from East Berlin – and at goodness knows what risk to himself. And now he had travelled a hundred miles to help me again.

I smiled at him with heartfelt apology. 'You've been so good to me, Kurt, and I'm abominably self-centred. Were you in trouble when you got back to your office?'

He grimaced. 'There was a hue and cry, I can tell you! Fortunately I was back soon after they discovered that you were missing, and no one was able to prove that I had been away. And then, no one knew about the spare key I had. Ullstein held the key to the room you were in, so he's in real trouble.'

'Serves him right,' I said vindictively. I could still feel the bruises on my upper arm where he had gripped me. 'But how did you manage to get away again?'

'Oh . . . I just went . . .'

'And when you get back?'

'There will be trouble,' he confirmed. 'But all I'm concerned with at the moment is getting you out of here.

You're still with the Americans? Good. I came to tell you that I have some contacts among the border guards not far from here, and I'll be able to get you across late tonight. I'll arrange for someone to meet you on the other side and take you to the nearest British consulate.'

'Oh Kurt, you really have been wonderful! I've said thank you, half a dozen times, and it's so inadequate . . . but – what about Nicolas?'

He gave me a level look. 'That's entirely my affair, I think. If he's in Marberg I certainly intend to find him.'

'And then what?'

'That depends. Tell me, are you still in love with him?'

I drew a long, shuddering breath.

Well? Was I? Wasn't it time, after the way Nicolas had treated me, to ignore the totally irrational response of my heart and start using my head?

I lifted my chin. 'No,' I said.

He nodded, slowly. 'I'm glad. You deserve someone better. And this makes it easier for me to ask you for your help. If you still loved him, even after the way he has treated you, I couldn't ask you this. But now, will you please help me to find him? I can't be sure of recognising him, you see, especially if he's wearing some kind of disguise.'

I hesitated.

'You did say that thanks were inadequate,' Kurt reminded me gently.

'What – what exactly are you going to do when you find him?'

'Oh, don't worry – I'm not proposing to do him any injury! But I want to find out what he meant by betraying you, and I must know what he's up to here in Marberg. If he can use you as he did, then God knows who else he might be intent on harming. Don't you see, my dear, he's not to be trusted? We must stop him before he does any more damage to innocent people.'

It made sense. I didn't want to believe any of it, but the facts were irrefutable. Nicolas might not love me, but he had known me for years. If *I* couldn't trust him, then no one could.

Kurt was right. Whatever Nicolas was doing, he would have to be stopped.

I nodded. 'I suppose so,' I said dully.

'I felt sure that you would understand.' Kurt looked at his watch. 'I have to make the arrangements now for getting you across the border, so I must leave you for an hour or two. Perhaps you could join your American friends and tell them that all is well, and then come up to the town this afternoon? If Allen is in costume, I imagine that he intends to be there. I shall be waiting for you at the main gate at three o'clock, and then we'll watch the performers. I'll make it as easy for you as possible, I promise – I don't want you to speak to Allen or touch him, just point him out to me if you see him. Will you do that?'

I bit my lip. To agree to give away – to betray – Nicolas was unthinkable. And yet, what had Nicolas ever done for me but betray me, literally and emotionally? I owed him nothing.

But to Kurt – kind, solid, reassuring Kurt – my debt was incalculable. He was fond of me, possibly even a little in love with me, and all I had given him in return were constant reminders that I was in love with Nicolas, a man we both had good reason to mistrust. This was my opportunity – my one opportunity before he arranged for me to be smuggled back across the border to safety – to show my thanks to Kurt for everything. I couldn't not take it.

I closed my eyes and swallowed hard. 'Yes,' I promised.

CHAPTER 18

Scott came bounding up to me as I sleepwalked my way through the camp site.

'You found Nicolas, then,' he stated. 'I saw you with him near the entrance as I came back from the town.'

I tried to sort out in my mind what he was talking about, and then recalled seeing him pass by at a moment when I was in Kurt's arms. The conclusion he had come to was understandable, and since I couldn't possibly tell the boy the whole truth, there was no point in confusing him by trying to explain that Kurt wasn't Nicolas.

'Er – yes,' I agreed. I made a painful sketch of a smile. 'Everything's all right now. We'll be leaving tonight.'

Disappointment tossed with relief for possession of Scott's cherubic face, and relief won. 'Oh, that's great! I mean – ' he pushed the curls off his forehead, embarrassed, 'I'm sorry you're going before we leave, of course, but it's really good to know that you'll have no more trouble. I just couldn't figure out how I was going to get you across the border without your papers! Where's Nicolas now?'

'Oh . . . he had to go back to the town. I'm meeting him up there this afternoon. I – I really came back just to say goodbye to everyone.'

I could hear the unsteadiness in my voice and I knew that I couldn't trust myself to say much more. My emotions were too near the surface.

Scott was peering at me, his forehead wrinkling with perplexity. 'Are you *sure* everything's all right, Alison?'

'Yes – yes of course.'

'It *is*? So why are you crying?'

'I'm not – ' I began, then pushed past him and hurried on, holding my head high to keep the treacherous tears from overflowing.

Scott sighed and fell into step beside me. 'I guess,' he announced gloomily, 'that I'll just never understand women.'

*

I splashed my face with cold water in the shower block, and then went to say my farewells and thanks to Nancy and Paul and the others. I felt numbed now. If I let myself think of Nicolas I should be in tears again, so I kept my tumultuous emotions firmly battened down and concentrated all my ability on entertaining them with bright, frivolous conversation while we shared a picnic lunch.

Before we parted, Scott insisted that we exchange addresses. After a moment's thought, I gave him my home address in Leicester. That, after all, was where I should be going as soon as I returned to England. I never wanted to see Norfolk again.

I smiled at the boy. 'Goodbye – and thank you for all your help.' I leaned forward and kissed him lightly on the cheek, and he blushed with embarrassed gratification.

'You're welcome,' he mumbled.

I gave the Americans time to get clear before I followed them up to the town. They had been wonderfully good to me and I didn't want them to be involved any further. As I approached the main gate, Kurt stepped out of the shadows.

'Thank you for coming, my dear. I was half afraid – '

'I promised,' I pointed out flatly.

'Yes.' He took my arm, looking down at me with affectionate concern. 'I'm so glad that you understand. It really is important that we find Allen – you know from your own experience how little he is to be trusted.'

His fingers tightened. 'Don't worry, I'll have you safely back in the West this evening, and then you'll be able to forget this whole wretched business.'

I doubted that, but it seemed ungrateful to say so.

As we walked through the gateway, I caught a sudden glimpse of Scott. As soon as he saw us he started, reddened, and hared away. Possibly he'd been lingering to make sure that I really was being met, and was now reassured. Gallant to the last, I thought affectionately.

Kurt kept my arm in his as we walked through the town, either because he liked the contact or to prevent us from being separated by the crowds. Either way, I acquiesced. Quite apart from the tourists, every inhabitant of the Upper Harz region seemed to have come crowding into Marberg for the festival, and I didn't want to lose Kurt. He was my rescuer, my lifeline to the free world, and I was glad to cling to him.

We reached the market place and edged on to the steps of the town hall. A lively folk dance was taking place in front of the dais where the great cask of wine would eventually stand.

'Any sign of Allen?' Kurt asked impatiently.

'Not as far as I can see.'

'He was in a procession, you said? Let's go and find it.'

It wasn't far to the castle, but it took some time to get there because the crowds were even thicker. The procession hadn't yet started. The doors of the castle were still closed and guarded by Volkspolizei, and the oxen, garlanded with wild flowers for their performance, stood yoked to the empty waggon, waiting to enter.

Here, in front of the castle, every other person seemed to be in costume of some kind. The chances of identifying Nicolas would be minimal. Perhaps he wasn't even here...

I was too confused to be certain whether I wanted to see him or not. If he didn't come, or if I simply couldn't find him, then there would be no dilemma. My natural, cowardly instincts told me that this was what I must hope for.

But emotionally, of course, I longed to see him. I couldn't really bring myself to believe that he had abandoned me. If I could see him again, and if he smiled at me in recognition, I should know at once that everything that had made me mistrust him – my being picked up in Berlin, his blank stare when I saw him this morning – had been a terrible mistake. It could all so easily be put right, I felt sure.

But supposing I did see him now, this afternoon, and received nothing but another blank stare?

If that happened . . . if that happened, then it would in effect be an admission of his guilt. If that happened, I told myself fiercely, I would ignore my heart's foolishness and point out Nicolas to Kurt so that Kurt could deal with him. It would be the only possible, the only right thing for me to do. Nicolas had treated me abominably, and he deserved everything he would get from Kurt. I felt angry, vindictive.

Kurt had pushed our way through to one of the fountains that were such a feature of the streets of Marberg. This one had a square stone basin several feet high, with a central column that cascaded pink and white geraniums rather than water. A number of spectators had climbed on to the basin to get a better view, and Kurt lifted me up to join them. I sat on the stone edge looking over the heads of the crowd to the castle doors, steadying myself with one hand on Kurt's shoulder.

The Vopos who seemed to be on permanent guard outside the castle's great doors once again moved aside. The doors were opened, the waggon rumbled through and a dozen or so costumed men followed it to load up the wine cask in the castle courtyard. Then the drums began to beat and the fifes shrilled high above the cheers of the crowd as the oxen, blinking tolerantly through their garlands, came swaying back into view.

This was a holiday, a festival, a rare opportunity

for the local inhabitants to forget that they were prisoners in their own country, and they seemed to be in a mood to make the most of it. Impromptu dances were danced, hats and arms were flung in the air. The spectators swung their shoulders and stamped their feet to the music, and pushed their way forward to tack on to the end of the procession as it made its way past the fountain in the direction of the market place. As it passed I recognised the parti-coloured jester and the fat man in the buff jerkin, but there was small chance of identifying Nicolas even if he were –

There!

He was there, in the procession just as he had been this morning, wearing the same short dark blue cloak slung across one shoulder and the same broad-brimmed hat. Everyone taking part in the procession was looking among the spectators to identify and wave to friends, and Nicolas was looking about him too, but covertly; almost, I thought, anxiously.

Looking, perhaps, for me?

He was level with me, no more than fifteen feet away. I stared at him longingly, willing him to see me, but not daring to do anything to attract his attention. I had to keep my knowledge from Kurt until I had seen Nicolas's reaction.

He would smile when he saw me, I knew he would. The rapid beat of my heart confirmed that this was all I wanted: one smile of recognition from Nicolas and then I would simply deny to Kurt that I had seen him. Nicolas was obviously here on business of his own, and once we were safely back in England there would be plenty of opportunity to sort out all the mistakes and misunderstandings.

He was almost past. He still hadn't seen me. Furtively, desperately, I raised the hand furthest from Kurt and waved it. Nicolas turned his head towards me. Our eyes met.

He recognised me. There was absolutely no doubt about that. Even fifteen feet away across the bobbing heads of the merrymaking citizens of Marberg, I could see the light of recognition in his eyes.

I was smiling at him now, waving frantically, awaiting his response.

None came. His face remained cold, impassive, his eyes slid away, he walked on.

'You've seen him? Where is he?' Kurt was shaking my arm urgently and I realised that my fingers – resting at first so lightly on his shoulder – were now gripping him fiercely. There would be no point in trying to deny that I had seen Nicolas.

Even if I wanted to.

But as for betraying him . . .

No. Whatever Kurt told me, whatever reason told me, I couldn't do it. Even though Nicolas had deserted me and left me desolate, I couldn't hate him enough to give him away.

My voice was thick with tears. 'He's there,' I choked, pointing to a complete stranger at the head of the procession: 'There, the one in the red cloak!'

'Well done, my dear – thank you!' Kurt loosened my fingers and patted my hand, all without taking his eyes from the red cloak as its wearer moved on. 'You stay here,' he commanded, 'and don't worry about anything. I'll come back and fetch you later, after I've had it out with Allen.'

Kurt pushed his way forward, finding as I had found that he was caught up and delayed by the spectators who crowded in the wake of the procession. I stood up on the stone basin of the fountain, hoping to catch a last glimpse of Nicolas, but he was already out of sight. The square was emptying rapidly as everyone was drawn by the music towards the market place, and I was left alone.

I scrambled down from the fountain, choking back my desolation, and ran. Anywhere, so long as it was away from both Kurt and Nicolas.

*

I didn't pause until I reached a gateway in the town walls, a small arch leading out to a little-used dirt road that wound down the hill and lost itself among the trees. I ran through the archway and then hesitated, bewildered, until I looked back and recognised the Dürer watch tower rearing high above the wall. This was the way Scott had brought me this morning.

There were several footpaths leading down into the woods, but I recognised one of the green tunnels and plunged down the steep zig-zag path that led to the camp site. One of the people who worked at the camp would be able to tell me where the coaches were parked, and if I found his coach I would eventually find Willy Hendricks.

It would be a lot to ask of him, of course, but I couldn't believe that Willy would refuse to help me. If Kurt had contacts who could get me across the border then surely Willy, who had relatives in Marberg, would be able to do the same.

If I'd stopped to consider, I might have known that it wouldn't be as easy as that to cross the border. If it were, half the population of Marberg would have hopped over long since.

But I couldn't begin to think coherently. I needed urgently to get away, to escape from this walled-in town and this terrifyingly wired-in country, and I wanted to do it without the humiliation of seeing either Nicolas or Kurt ever again.

Anxiety made me try to run too quickly along the tree-shadowed path. I leaped over a fallen branch that lay in my way, slipped on a patch of muddy ground and fell. As I stumbled to my feet and brushed my skirt I heard, unmistakably, the sound of someone sliding and pushing through the undergrowth just above me and a little to my right.

I held my breath and listened. The noise stopped.

I ran on, straining to hear, and the sounds came again. Someone else was hurrying down the hill, slithering down one of the steeper paths that ran almost straight from top to bottom. I stopped in mid-stride but the noise was ahead of me now, going on down.

I breathed more easily. For just a moment I had been afraid that I was being followed, that Kurt was chasing me to exact revenge for the way I had deceived him.

Telling myself sharply not to imagine things, I ran on to the next elbow of the path. This was the place where the hillside levelled a little and the trees thinned, the grassy place where Scott and I had rested on the way up.

I rested for a minute now, propping myself at arm's length against an oak tree that grew at the edge of the path, deliberately giving the other runner time to get clear. I listened again. The foot of the hill was still some way below, and I could hear nothing more. I shrugged, and pushed myself upright.

Just behind me, the bushes rustled.

Fear made my scalp prickle. I turned my head.

Nothing.

And then, from the other side, a man rushed me. I whirled round to face him, terrified, a scream rising instinctively to my lips, but he pulled me roughly to him and clapped his hand over my mouth.

CHAPTER 19

I had never before seen his face so dark with anger. The green of his eyes was icy, contemptuous, his grip painful.

'Don't you dare scream,' he warned me in a low, hard voice. 'I'll take my hand away only if you're prepared to keep quiet. Are you?'

His hand was pressed over my nose and mouth, smothering me. I nodded as well as I could, gasping with relief as he took it away. He shifted his grip on my arms, looked round quickly and then hurried me across the clearing and behind the big linden tree out of sight of the path.

'Now!' said Nicolas grimly, grasping my shoulders and forcing me to face him. 'What the hell do you think you're doing?'

The adrenalin had flowed, turning fear into fury. '*You*,' I choked, '*you* have the nerve to ask me that! Considering what you did to me, what I've been through on your account . . . ' I gestured incoherently to the dark-blue cloak that was still slung across his shoulder, 'considering that I didn't point you out, even though it meant breaking my promise to Kurt . . . '

He shook his head impatiently. 'I haven't the faintest idea what you're talking about! And for heaven's sake keep your voice down. You don't imagine that I'm dressed up for fun, do you? I came here on a special mission and it's vital that I'm accepted as one of the local population – and there you were at the rehearsal this morning, doing your very best to give me away!

You'd have succeeded too, if I hadn't spotted you in the crowd just before you saw me. I was really shaken – I'd assumed that you were safely back in England. What do you mean by coming here? Why in heaven's name didn't you do as you were told and go straight back to West Berlin?'

I was quivering with anger. 'How can you ask me that? You were the one who gave *me* away! If it hadn't been for Kurt – let go, Nicolas, you're hurting me.'

He slackened his grip a little. 'You've become extraordinarily friendly with Braun, haven't you?' he demanded. 'I wasted precious time this morning following you down to the camp site in the hope of being able to speak to you in private, and there you were in his arms. And then this afternoon you were wandering round the town together arm in arm. Why did he bring you here? What are you both up to?'

I ducked suddenly, wriggling out of his grasp, and stood glaring at him. My hands trembled as I pushed the hair away from my face.

'Kurt,' I said with dignity, 'has been wonderfully good and kind and helpful – which is a great deal more than I can say of you! I hated you for what you did to me, but I still couldn't give you away to him because I thought he was going to beat you up. But now . . . if I'd known how oafish you were going to be . . . I wish I *had* given you away. It would serve you right if he did beat you up. You're the most callous, inconsiderate –'

'Stop being so ridiculously melodramatic, Alison. If Braun wants to beat me up he's welcome to try – but why on earth should he want to?'

'Because you gave me away to the East Germans, of course,' I snapped. 'It was a wicked, despicable thing to do – as Kurt says, you're obviously not to be trusted –'

Nicolas's expression had been slowly changing from angry contempt to incredulity: '*I* gave you away to the . . . Alison, what are you talking about?'

His horrified disbelief was so completely genuine that I felt a sudden, overwhelming welling-up of relief. Then

Kurt had been mistaken about Nicolas – and so, thank heaven, had I!

What had happened in East Berlin had nothing to do with Nicolas at all. It was almost certainly, I thought, the porter in the apartment block who had given me away. I found myself telling Nicolas so, babbling out the whole story up to the point where Kurt had come to Marberg.

I had never seen anyone with such a shattered look. Nicolas listened in silence, shaking his head with anxiety at intervals.

'Oh, Alison . . . you poor girl! If I'd had any idea that this would happen . . . it seemed so simple, and Braun guaranteed the arrangement on this side. I can't begin to tell you how sorry I am.'

'Well, it was my own stupid fault,' I admitted. 'Kurt warned me about that porter, but I really gave myself away by chatting to her. And you'd told me not to take anything over with me, but I insisted on taking my own lipstick. So I can't blame anyone else.'

'Even so . . . I can only thank heaven that Braun was there to look after you. But, Alison – even though he might have been suspicious of my intentions, I still don't understand how *you* could seriously imagine that I would give you away to the East Germans! Why didn't you use your common sense? My family knows and likes you, and we know your aunt. What did you expect me to do? Go back to England and say to my mother, "Oh, by the way, I've left Alison over in East Germany and it's bound to be a few years before they let her out of prison, so perhaps you'll mention it to her aunt next time you see her . . . "? Of *course* I didn't give you away.' He gave a wry grimace. 'You must have had a very poor opinion of me to imagine that I could ever do such a thing.'

I shrugged. 'When you're stuck behind the East German frontier,' I pointed out, 'it's difficult to think kindly of the man who was responsible for putting you there.'

He groaned. 'I know . . . I can hardly expect you to

forgive me easily for what has happened to you. But frankly, Alison, I don't believe that you gave yourself away. Elisabeth would never have been allowed to go to the West if they'd suspected her. There must have been some other reason for picking you up.'

'Does it matter, now?' I was conscious, now that I was safe, of an overwhelming weariness. The whole wretched affair was incomprehensible. I didn't want to have to think about it any more.

Nicolas checked his watch. 'Of course it does,' he said abruptly. 'If someone arranged for you to be picked up, I have to know who and why. It certainly wasn't anyone in the West, so I'm beginning to wonder in Braun had a hand in it.'

'Kurt? Don't be ridiculous!'

'It's not ridiculous,' he said sternly. 'Tell me – you said that Braun was surprised that you had seen me here?'

'Every bit as surprised as I was. He did say that you probably had some business of your own here, but he had no idea what it was.'

Nicolas frowned. 'Well, that's not true for a start. He certainly didn't know for sure that I was coming, but he must have guessed. He'd know perfectly well *why* I was here.'

'Why?' I asked.

He looked at me reprovingly. 'I thought I'd trained you not to ask questions. Look, you say that Braun persuaded the driver of a West German coach to bring you here – Willy Hendricks, by any chance?'

'Yes. Kurt said that Willy was one of his West German contacts.'

'So he is. Willy is one of our men, as Braun knows. But Braun didn't ask Willy to help you across the border?'

'Well, no. But he explained why. Willy has relatives in Marberg and it was too much of a risk for him. Kurt said that I wasn't to ask Willy for help, except as the very last resort.'

Nicolas's eyes narrowed. 'Did he . . . ? Then I'm sorry, but that proves that Braun has been misleading you.'

I was indignant. 'I don't believe it! He was being considerate, that's all – he tried not to involve Willy unnecessarily.'

'Rubbish. Involvement is part of Willy's job. If Braun had really wanted to help you in East Berlin, he would have told Willy the whole story and put you in his care. There was no need for Braun to come here at all – besides, he couldn't get you across the border.'

'I don't see why not – presumably you're planning to get across yourself?'

'And taking you with me! But we've had to set up a complex operation to do it, because there are no roads across the border in this region at all. It's wired and mined and guarded all the way, and Braun knows it.'

I was too weary to argue. 'I don't know what his plans are, do I?' I said irritably. 'All I know is that Kurt has been marvellously kind to me and I won't hear a word against him. I'm going up to the town now to find him and tell him that everything's all right, and that he doesn't have to look for you any more.'

Nicolas went very still. 'Look for me, did you say?'

'Yes, that's what he's doing. That's why he wanted me to point you out to him when I saw you, because he wasn't entirely sure of recognising you. We thought we couldn't trust you, you see, and that you'd have to be stopped from doing . . . whatever you are doing. But as soon as I explain to him that it's all been a terrible misunderstanding – '

'No!' Nicolas was decisive. 'You're explaining nothing to him and you're certainly not going looking for him!'

I stared at him blankly. 'But Nicolas, I must! I have to tell him that I've found you and that you'll be taking me across the border – and I certainly have to thank him for everything he's done for me. Good heavens, without him I'd be in an East German prison now! He's been marvellous – and he's really rather a dear. He would be terribly hurt if I didn't say goodbye –'

Nicolas scowled. 'You don't know what you're talking about,' he snapped.

'I most certainly do! What's the matter with you, Nicolas? A few minutes ago you seemed as full of gratitude to him as I am.'

'Well, I've changed my mind. I'm not sure about him any more. You stay here, and wait for me.'

I was livid. 'I shall do nothing of the kind. Don't you dare order me about, after what I've been through for you . . . All right, so you didn't give me away to the East Germans, I'd have realised that if I'd been able to think straight. But you knew that there was a risk in sending me across the Berlin Wall, and you didn't worry about that, did you? Kurt said that no man who . . . he said that *he* would never send a girl across the Wall, it's too dangerous. And now you have the nerve to say that you don't trust him –'

I knew that my voice was rising in anger, and I didn't care. For a few minutes I had let myself bask in the knowledge that Nicolas hadn't betrayed me, and I'd felt all my love for him returning. If he had been gentle and sympathetic, the kind of man Kurt was, I would have been only too glad at that moment to shelter behind him and do as he asked. But I was far too overwrought to accept authority from a man who obviously cared so little for me.

Nicolas had been putting a finger to his lips, trying to shush me. Now he grabbed at my wrists.

'Let me go!' I shouted, struggling to free myself. 'Let me go – you're hurting –'

He clapped his hand over my lips again, but too late. My shouts had been heard. His body jerked and his mouth opened in surprise as someone rushed him from the back, wrapping both arms tightly round his throat.

*

Nicolas's reaction was immediate and frightening. He

took one step backwards, his hands went up to the arms twisted round his neck, he bent forward and someone, all arms and legs and tumbling curls, came flying over his shoulder to land with a sickening thud on the grass beside me.

And lay still.

'Scott!' I sank down on my knees beside the body. 'Scott . . . ' I looked up, my eyes half-blind with horror. 'Oh my God Nicolas, you've killed him!'

Nicolas was staring in surprise and dismay. 'No I haven't,' he snapped, pushing me aside and kneeling by the boy. 'He's winded, that's all. Is this the American boy you were telling me about? What the devil did he think he was doing, jumping me like that – I might have broken half the bones in his body.'

Scott's face was deathly white and his pulse was erratic but he was indisputably alive. I brushed the hair tenderly out of his eyes.

'I think,' I said shakily, 'that he was probably trying to protect me. I told him that I'd seen you in the town, and then he saw me with Kurt and assumed that *he* was Nicolas. It seemed too complicated to explain, so I didn't try. Scott must have been coming down the path from the town to the camp, heard us arguing and thought that I was being attacked by a stranger.'

'That was chivalrous of him. He's got plenty of pluck, I'll say that. Ah, he seems to be coming round.'

Scott's lashes fluttered, then flew open. For a second he stared at me uncomprehendingly, and then recognition returned.

'Are you okay?' he mumbled thickly.

'It's all right, Scott dear,' I said. 'I'm with Nicolas – this is Nicolas. The other man was . . . someone else. Are you hurt?'

In the circumstances it was a stupid question. The boy was too dazed and shaken to be able to assess the state of his health. Nicolas made a more practical approach.

'Sorry about that, friend,' he said. 'Look, can you

turn your head from side to side? Good. What about trying to move your arms, one at a time . . . slowly does it . . . that's fine. Now your legs.' He was very gentle with the boy, calm and competent. 'Does that hurt? Or that? Good, I don't seem to have damaged you, though you'll have some painful bruises.'

'He has a nasty cut on the side of his head,' I pointed out, tenderly investigating some of the matted, darkened curls.

'Hmm – we could see better if we cleaned that up a bit. I think I can hear running water over there. You'd better stay here, Alison, you're almost as pale as he is. I can look after him – besides I owe him that much. Come on then, bold Sir Lancelot, let's have you.'

Scott was still too shaky to stand unaided and Nicolas heaved him up in a fireman's lift and carried him through the bushes towards the sound of the water. I sat down thankfully on the grass under the linden tree, and closed my eyes.

The fright of seeing Scott lying, as I thought, dead, had shaken me more than I realised. I felt emotionally and physically exhausted. I was no longer able to think clearly or take any positive action. I knew that, in all fairness and courtesy, I ought to go up to the town and find Kurt. The fact that Nicolas objected to my going did nothing to deter me, but at the moment I simply felt unable to make the effort.

From the side of the stream came sounds of spluttering and coughing and a sudden heartening yelp of protest. Scott, it seemed, was recovering rapidly.

'Keep still a moment,' I heard Nicolas say. 'Ah, you've only grazed your head. You'll live.'

'Ouch, I ache all over,' Scott groaned. 'What happened?'

'You need to learn something about unarmed combat before you go round jumping on strange men,' Nicolas advised. 'But it was very brave of you to try to help Alison. I hear you've been a good friend to her, Scott.'

'Oh, I've enjoyed it – until five minutes ago, that is! I

thought that the other guy was Nicolas, you see. That was why I jumped you. It didn't seem quite right for him to be Nicolas, though. I mean, he was older, more responsible-looking – not the kind to let a girl down.'

My cheeks began to flame. Dear Scott – chatty to the last, he was obviously about to pour out all my troubles. I jumped to my feet, but the knock on his head must have loosened his tongue to such an extent that his words came tumbling out before I could even begin moving.

'I can understand it all now,' he was saying. 'I saw her right after she'd talked to him, and she said that everything was okay, but she was crying. Well, it didn't make sense for her to be crying over this nice steady grey-haired guy – and now I know that she wasn't. You're the one she's been crying over!'

His voice became indignant, excitable. 'She loves you, you know that? She really loves you – even after the way you treated her, bringing her over to East Germany and then leaving her without any papers and all. She was worried sick. But she still went right on loving you, and I reckon that's a whole lot more than you deserve. I – I'd like to punch you on the nose for the way you've been hurting Alison!'

I sat down abruptly, crimson with embarrassment. If there had been a rabbit hole handy, I swear I'd have tried to dig my way down it.

'Calm down,' Nicolas was saying in a friendly voice, 'it's no use your throwing punches until you're steadier than that on your feet, now is it? I can understand the way you feel, though. I *have* treated Alison badly, very badly indeed, and I'm going to apologise to her properly the minute I get the chance.'

Scott sounded slightly mollified. 'We-ll . . . I still don't see how you could let her wander about in East Germany without you. Not in *East* Germany of all places.'

There came what seemed like a long silence. I sat very still, looking out across the rolling wooded hills, hearing the plash and ripple of water and the intoxicated buzzing above me, and breathing the slow-dropping honeyed scent of the linden flowers.

Then I heard Nicolas speaking again, quietly and thoughtfully: 'No, I suppose it's hardly credible that I'd do that to anyone I was fond of. But you see, when I planned this trip to East Germany with Alison, I hardly knew her. How did I know that I was going to fall in love with her?'

CHAPTER 20

I watched Nicolas as he walked towards me, but his look was entirely preoccupied. He hadn't realised that I had overheard, and I was glad of it.

He stopped a few feet from me and looked at his watch. 'Scott will be perfectly all right,' he said. 'I've told him to stay there quietly for a while, but there's no need to worry about him. He did remind me though, that I have a lot of apologising and explaining to do to you.'

I muttered something noncommittal, but he didn't listen.

'I still have my mission to finish,' he said, 'and I must get back to the town. But first, I think you've every right to know what I've been doing, and why.'

'That would be a help,' I said shakily.

He sat down on the grass beside me, but not too close. He hardly glanced at me as he spoke, which was just as well or I would never have been able to concentrate.

'I've come to Marberg,' he told me, 'to help Elisabeth's father escape to the West.'

'Dr Lorenz? But I thought he was ill?'

'He had a breakdown about a year ago, but he recovered completely. He's as normal now as any of us – though God knows how long that will last if they keep him locked up in Marberg Castle.'

'In Marberg . . . in the castle up there?'

'Yes. Officially it's classed as a mental hospital, but prison might be a better word for it. You must have heard of the infamous practice in the Soviet Union of putting political prisoners in mental hospitals in order to destroy their resistance? This is what the East Germans are trying to do to Dr Lorenz.'

I remembered my sense of foreboding as I passed under the grim walls of the castle, and the glimpse I had had, across the courtyard, of white faces pressed against windows.

'But that's terrible,' I protested. '*Why*, Nicolas? Why is Dr Lorenz a political prisoner at all?'

He shrugged coldly. 'For the usual reason in any police state. He objected to living under a régime that denied him freedom of conscience, and he said so. As it happens, he has an international reputation in his particular field of medical research, and he has English friends in high places, so his criticisms of the East German régime carried weight. He was invited to an important medical congress in Stockholm last year, when he was going to give details of his research, but the government was afraid to let him go because of the bad publicity they knew he would give them. It was after his visa was refused – which meant that the details of his research would never become freely available to the whole world – that he had his breakdown. This was used as an excuse to put him in an institution and he's been there ever since, rotting away.'

I felt sickened. 'That's abominable . . . But does Elisabeth know what you're doing? You said that she didn't want to leave East Germany.'

'That's true. She herself was perfectly happy – she'd never known what life was like anywhere other than in a Communist State, and she quarrelled bitterly with her father. But when his visa was refused and he became ill, she obviously had second thoughts. And when she visited him at the castle and discovered the true situation, she decided to try to help get him out.'

'And that was why you wanted to see her in West Berlin?'

'Yes. One of her father's friends is a contact of mine and he helped to make the arrangements for the escape. But it's impossible for anyone except close relatives to visit the castle, and then only infrequently, and we couldn't plan the operation until we knew its layout.'

And now I understood. 'So you used her visit to her grandmother to ask her about the details of the castle!'

'Exactly. But to expect Elisabeth to spend the precious few minutes of her official visit talking to me, when she wanted to be with her grandmother, was inhuman. Then I saw you at the theatre, realised the resemblance, and devised the switch so that Elisabeth could stay longer in the West. The switch was the only part of the operation Braun knew about, and he assured me that there would be no trouble in East Berlin. We've worked in co-operation often enough, so of course I believed him – otherwise I'd never have let you come across.'

I frowned absently at a blade of grass I had pulled. 'But now you think that he isn't reliable?'

'I'm sure of it, after what you told me. You and I are not both here at the same time by coincidence, Alison. Braun brought you here for a very good reason.'

I tossed the grass away. 'What, for goodness' sake?' I demanded.

He hesitated before answering. 'I'm not known by sight to the intelligence people over here in the East,' he said. 'Normally I work either in West Berlin or in London. I was put on this particular mission because I once met Dr Lorenz and so he knows and trusts me – and that's important if I'm to get him out of the castle safely. I think that Braun guessed that I would be coming here, and when, and that he wants to take advantage of it.'

'You mean – he's changed sides? He wants to stop your mission?'

'Yes, I think he may have turned. He certainly wouldn't be the first agent – on either side – to do so. But if the East Germans wanted to stop the mission, they'd have much simpler ways of doing it than sending Braun all the way from Berlin. No – ' he gave me a small, crooked grin, ' – at the risk of seeming bumptious,

I rather think that he may be interested in me personally. And from what you said, I'm sure that he set you up to help him.'

My throat tightened. 'You mean,' I whispered, 'that Kurt has been *using* me? But that's impossible! He's been the one who has helped me!'

'If I'm right, all he's been doing is to win you over to his side by helping you out of dangerous situations that were entirely of his own contriving. Look, Alison –' Nicolas reached out and took my hand, clasping it strongly in his own as he spoke, ' – I know that you've had a very rough time and that you feel grateful to Braun, but believe me, if the Vopos really had picked you up, you'd never have got away. I think that all the terrifying things you've been through were deliberately staged by Braun, or his masters, in order to frighten you and make you indebted to him for what you thought was his help. He sent you here because he could be pretty sure that if I was in Marberg, you'd find me. He also knew that I couldn't possibly acknowledge you in public, because it would endanger my mission. I think he believed that this would turn you against me so effectively that you would be prepared, in revenge, to point me out to him. And it almost worked, didn't it?'

'Don't, Nicolas!' I pulled my hand away and turned my head from him in an attempt to conceal my shame. Because now that I was safe with Nicolas, I could see exactly what Kurt had been doing. He'd tried one of the oldest dramatic devices in the book, one that playwrights have used for centuries – and although I was an actress, I'd been too overwrought to recognise it.

Kurt had been cunning. He had known that, once I was alone in Germany, I would be so terrified, so dependent on him that I would believe him implicitly. Kurt, with his kindness and sympathy, had persuaded me to mistrust Nicolas – for a few moments, even to hate him. Almost, to hate him enough to betray him.

Wasn't there a couplet in a scene from a Restoration drama that we'd once learned at Drama School, a couplet that expressed the conflict exactly? . . . 'Heaven has no rage like love to hatred turned –'

' "Nor hell a fury like a woman scorned." '

I hardly knew that I had whispered the last line aloud, but suddenly Nicolas was kneeling in front of me, gently taking my face between his hands. His eyes were serious, his voice remorseful:

'And you thought that you were a woman scorned – that *I'd* scorned you? Oh, my sweet love . . . And yet you still didn't give me away? You've been wonderful, Alison – I don't deserve ever to be forgiven.'

His lips were so near that there was only one possible form of reply. I was floating, conscious of nothing but 'Oh my sweet love' and the taste of his mouth, unable to imagine, in that moment out of time, that there could be anything to forgive.

*

Abruptly, breathlessly, he pulled himself away and stood up.

'I'm sorry, Alison,' he said, his voice jerky, 'but I have to go. I'd like to say: "To hell with everyone else" and stay with you here under this linden tree until it's time for us to leave, but I can't. Not when a man's life and work – and the lives of all the people he can help through his work – depend on what I do in the next hour. It must seem very unflattering to you and I apologise, but I must finish what I came here to do.'

I wasn't interested in flattery. Besides, I'd been through too much to want to see it all go to waste. 'I understand,' I said.

'That's what I hoped. Now listen.' He drew a deep breath, and his voice steadied. 'I must get back to the town. I'm supposed to be in the market place at the moment, establishing the fact that I'm part of the procession so that I can help with the job of returning the wine cask to the castle. Don't ask me how I'm going to get Dr Lorenz out, because there's no need for you to know. It's all carefully timed and planned, and there's a getaway car hidden among the trees just off the dirt road at the top of this path. I want you to stay here while I do my job and then go up the path and be waiting out of sight near the car in an hour's time, at seven-fifteen. Right?'

I nodded. We checked watches, and then Nicolas picked his hat out of the bushes where he had flung it when he jumped me, and adjusted his short cloak across his shoulder.

For a few seconds we stood looking at each other. The thundering of my blood was so loud in my ears that it drowned even the sound of the bees, but the linden flowers were sweeter than ever, their scent pervading my senses.

Nicolas bent his head towards me and I raised my face, but he only smiled, cupping it between his large hands and kissing my forehead. 'Let's not risk starting anything,' he advised, 'not before I get you back to safety. And please do as I say, and stay hidden beside the car – you've run enough risks already.'

Suddenly, as if remembering what I had been through, he seized me and held me close and for a moment I clung to him, feeling the strong slow hammer of his heart against mine.

'Be careful,' I whispered, and then I wrenched myself away. 'Go on then, if you're going . . . ' I said unsteadily.

He rescued his absurd hat from the ground where it had fallen, blew the dust off it, touched my cheek with his fingers, gave me a lop-sided grin and then set off at a steady lope along the zig-zag path and up the hill towards Marberg.

*

I had completely forgotten Scott. Remembering him now, I pushed through the bushes and found him sitting beside a spring. He climbed slowly to his feet, looking guilty and defiant as I approached.

'How are you?' I asked.

'Fine now, thanks, Alison.' He hesitated, and then

said it in a rush: 'I hate to tell you this, but I overheard what you and Nicolas were saying. I wasn't deliberately eavesdropping, I promise, and I didn't *look* – but I heard what Nicolas was saying about the man in the castle, and about the grey-haired guy and everything. I know I ought not to have listened, but I felt too groggy to move away. I'm very sorry.'

Considering that I had heard every word of his conversation with Nicolas, I could hardly blame him. 'You couldn't help it, Scott,' I said quickly. 'But you do realise that it was all very confidential? It's most important that you don't tell anyone why Nicolas is here.'

He squirmed impatiently. 'Of *course* I won't,' he affirmed. 'I mean, I shan't see anyone to tell, anyway. I'm going to stay right here with you until you leave with Nicolas in that car. Hey, he *is* an intelligence agent, isn't he?'

I smiled at the gleam of excitement in his eyes, and evaded his question. 'I'll certainly be glad of your company, Scott,' I said, 'if you really don't mind staying, but I think I'll go and look for the car now, and hide near it. I don't want to get involved in anything else.'

Scott moved stiffly at first as we went up the path, but his encounter with Nicolas seemed to be a source of pride rather than indignation. To have been flattened by a real live intelligence agent, and to have the bruises to show for it, was clearly going to be a better story to take home than the one about lending his tent to a destitute actress.

We found the car, well-hidden among trees and bushes at the side of the dirt road that led down from the Dürer watch tower towards the valley. The dusty road was deserted. This was obviously a comparatively little-used gate in the town walls and at the moment, judging from the distant sounds of music, the entire population was enjoying the festivities in the market place. It seemed that Nicolas had chosen an ideal time for springing Dr Lorenz from the castle.

We concealed ourselves behind some bushes. Scott lay

beside me on his stomach, peering through the foliage towards the stone gateway, tense with excitement. Given half a chance, I thought, he'd be off to join the action.

I was glad that I didn't know the details of what Nicolas was going to do. Obviously the castle had an armed police guard, festival or no festival, and smuggling Dr Lorenz out was going to be dangerous and difficult. But at least Nicolas hadn't Kurt to contend with as well –

I sat up, feeling my cheeks go cold as the blood drained from them. 'Oh dear heaven – !' I whispered.

Scott nudged me in alarm. 'What's the matter?'

My mouth had dried with fear. 'I'm an idiot!' I croaked. 'I never thought . . . Here I've been, smugly assuming that because I didn't give Nicolas away to Kurt, that's the end of that particular problem. But it isn't, of course! Nicolas is right, Kurt *is* after him. He told me in East Berlin that there were men on this side of the border who would very much like to get their hands on Nicolas, if only they could find him. And if they were prepared to go to the length of setting me up to point him out, then they must want him very badly. That means that Kurt will still be after him!'

Scott's eyes had rounded. 'You mean he wants to *kill* Nicolas?'

I shook my head. 'Worse, almost. He wants to take him in for questioning. Nicolas must have all kinds of information, and God knows what they'd be prepared to do to get it out of him. So Kurt's probably hanging round the castle now, waiting for Nicolas to break Dr Lorenz out. He'll recognise him then, he's bound to.'

Scott jumped to his feet. 'I'll go and warn Nicolas,' he said excitedly.

I leaped after him and hauled him back by the sleeve of his denim jacket. 'Don't be silly,' I snapped. 'Nicolas knows well enough what danger he's in – he had a very effective technique for taking my mind off the subject, that's all. No, you stay here. I'm going to see if I can find Kurt and head him off. I can persuade him that I made a mistake before, and that I know where Nicolas is, and then take him somewhere else.'

Scott stood tall, with his fists on his narrow hips. 'And then what will you do?' he demanded belligerently. 'Besides, Nicolas told you to stay here! *I'm* going to head off Kurt!'

'You're doing nothing of the sort – ' I began, but his eyes were sparkling as he looked up at the towers of the castle thrusting high above the walls of the town.

'How are you going to stop me?' he demanded.

I seized his hand and we both ran.

CHAPTER 21

The sun was low in the west and the narrow cobbled streets of Marberg were already in shadow as we hurried up into the town, but the windows high in the steep gables of the medieval houses winked and shone as they reflected the last golden brilliance of the day.

I made straight for the square in front of the castle. It was virtually deserted, apart from the two armed Vopos on guard outside the great closed doors. There was, though, another man standing discreetly behind the overflowing geraniums of the stone fountain.

'That's him,' whispered Scott excitedly as we peered round the massive carved wooden corner-post of one of the houses on the edge of the square. 'That's Braun. So he *is* up to something! I tell you what, Alison, they're going to bring that wine cask back to the castle and then Nicolas is probably going to smuggle the doctor out in the empty waggon! Or hanging underneath it, or something! Isn't this *great*?'

I was too tense to indulge him. Besides, he was no longer a child. 'No, it isn't!' I snapped. 'This isn't a game, Scott it's deadly serious. Look, will you please run up towards the market place and see if there's any sign of the waggon, and particularly of Nicolas? Only don't let him see you. He has enough on his mind at the moment without worrying about what you're up to.'

Scott sobered and raced off. He was back within minutes.

'It's what I thought,' he reported. 'The waggon's on its way back here with the cask, only there's no procession now. Everyone's living it up in the market place, apart from the half-dozen who are bringing the cask back. And Nicolas is one of 'em.'

I drew a deep breath. 'Right – ' I said.

Scott stared at me expectantly, waiting to hear my plan for drawing Kurt away; but the fact was that I had no plan. I knew what I had to do, but I was too much aware of the dangers involved to think coherently about the best way to do it. Fear churned my mind as it churned my stomach. All I could say to myself was: 'Oh, dear heaven, what am I going to do?' and 'Oh Nicolas . . . '

It wasn't that drawing Kurt away would be difficult. I might not be a brilliant actress, but at least I felt competent to convince him temporarily that Nicolas was elsewhere. The question was, what did I do with him once I got him away?

Give him the slip among the crowds in the market place? Perhaps. But the only result of that would be that he would suspect my intentions and return immediately to the castle. And I couldn't keep him occupied long enough to ensure that Nicolas and Dr Lorenz got away, because then I should be trapped myself. Nicolas might wait for me by the car, of course, but that would probably jeopardise his plan for getting across the border, and then all of us would be trapped . . .

Scott was watching me, frowning. His boyish excitement had been replaced by a wholly adult seriousness.

'I don't know if you'd like to hear my idea?' he offered diffidently.

Already we could see, at the far end of the street that led down from the market place, the slow rolling approach of the oxen. I listened as Scott quickly told me his plan. I didn't like it at all. It put him in considerable danger. But as he pointed out – with a new, masterly gleam in his eye – there was no time for me to argue.

'All right,' I agreed reluctantly. 'Only for goodness sake – '

He didn't wait to hear my injunction and I didn't

bother to finish it. We parted, speeding in different directions, and I had the satisfaction of seeing Kurt's mouth drop open in surprise as I raced up to him and seized his arm.

'Oh, Kurt,' I panted, 'thank goodness I've found you! I've been looking everywhere!'

'You have?' he asked suspiciously. 'Considering that you put me on to the wrong man this afternoon –'

I waved the matter aside impatiently. 'You don't imagine that was deliberate, do you? I realised my mistake immediately and called to you, but you didn't hear. So I followed Nicolas myself, and I know where he is now . . . Only you must hurry if you want to see him!'

He stared, uncertain. 'I've a pretty good idea that I'll be able to see him soon if I stay exactly where I am,' he said slowly.

I shook my head, acting the part of a scorned woman for all I was worth. 'But that's just what he wants you to think – I know now how devious he is! Oh Kurt, I don't know what he's up to, but he's treated me abominably and I want you to stop him from doing any more harm. He's hiding now in a little shed at the foot of one of the watch towers in the wall, waiting for someone or something. If we approach quietly along the wall you'll be able to take him by surprise – but we *must* hurry!'

I seized his arm. I was getting perilously close to hamming my part, but I could hear the rumble of the iron-bound wheels of the waggon and I knew that it would be in sight at any minute.

'Please, Kurt,' I begged. '*Please!*'

He glanced at the closed door of the castle and appeared to do a quick calculation. 'Which tower?' he asked.

'Oh – the fourth from here, clockwise, if we go up the nearest stairway.'

'Not far, then – it won't take long.' He made up his mind. 'All right, my dear, you lead the way and show me the shed where he's hiding just as soon as you see it.'

I ran for a stone stairway that Scott had pointed out

to me, in a corner of the square. It led twenty feet up to the wooden walkway on the inner side of the town walls, a gallery roofed with red tiles, that led from tower to tower.

Once on the top, I ran in the direction away from the castle, and the boards of the walkway juddered as Kurt Braun came belting after me.

One of the towers loomed up ahead, the first, conical capped. The walkway ended at a dark stone arch in the tower wall. I plunged through, then checked to adjust my eyes to the gloom. I was in a small bare circular room with stone walls and an uneven flagged floor; one steep spiral stairway led down through the thickness of the wall to the base of the tower and another up to the top, while a further arch in the opposite wall led out to the next walkway.

Kurt was close on my heels. I ran on to the next tower: number two. I was panting now, with fear as much as with exertion.

In the darkness of the second tower I stumbled and Kurt came closer. 'Can you see the shed yet?' he demanded.

I gestured ahead towards the next tower but one. The walls curved inward, giving a good view, but some houses hid the base of the fourth tower from sight. Just as well, I thought grimly. The shed was only a figment of Scott's imagination.

Kurt nodded, slipping his right hand inside his jacket, and motioned me on. It was a shorter distance to the next tower, the third. I took it as fast as I could, my feet bouncing off the boards, willing Kurt to follow me in a blind rush as he concentrated his attention on the fourth tower.

I took the last few feet from the walkway into the arch of the third in a single leap, flinging myself to one side as I entered the obscuring darkness. Kurt was coming after me, his face grim, his hand emerging from the shelter of his jacket. I saw him for a second, silhouetted against the light, with a gun in his raised hand. And then he had crossed the threshold and Scott went charging from beside me like a human cannonball, head down, and rammed into Kurt, knocking him off balance.

My gasp of warning to Scott coincided with the crack of the gun. There was an angry noise as the bullet ricocheted from wall to wall, a splat as it buried itself in the boards of the next walkway, a clatter as the gun hit the stone floor. I ducked instinctively, my hands to my face as dust showered and flakes of stone spat viciously within the confines of the tower room.

Kurt grunted something, his arms flailing as he tried to regain his balance. I could see his face in the gloom, contorted with rage. Scott was crouched near one wall. With a gathering roar of anger Kurt launched himself at the boy, who waited until the last possible moment before throwing himself out of Kurt's path.

The man's angry bellow changed its note as he saw what Scott's body had been concealing. He strode for an instant on air as the stone spiral stairway opened up beneath his feet and then he dropped, scraping and sliding and bouncing from wall to wall as he pitched from top to bottom.

*

Scott and I were late for the rendezvous with Nicolas, but I couldn't hurry. I felt dazed and cold and rather sick. I was bleeding from a gash on one arm where a flying stone had cut me.

Scott himself admitted to nothing more than a sore head. He was high on excitement and pride of achievement, and insisted on donating one of the cleaner parts of his shirt for the purpose of binding up my arm. Then he urged me on towards where the car was hidden, helping me along whenever I faltered.

There were two men already in the car, one in the driving seat and one in the back. Nicolas, without his fancy dress, stood waiting for me with a thunderous face.

'Where the hell have you been?' he stormed. 'Can't I

rely on you to do a single thing I tell you? And what have you been doing to yourself?'

I was still too shaken to be able to collect my wits sufficiently to give him the answer he deserved. Scott put a defensive arm around me and tried to explain, but Nicolas cut him short.

'There's no time to waste, I'll look at that arm later. A helicopter is picking us up this side of the border, and it won't be able to wait. You'd better come with us as far as the pick-up point, Scott. It'll be difficult enough to get Dr Lorenz aboard in a hurry, without having to look after Alison as well.'

I pulled myself together, indignant on Scott's behalf. 'But he can't leave Marberg,' I protested. 'You can't just use him and then leave him stranded! I'll be all right.'

'Of course I shan't leave him stranded,' Nicolas snapped. 'Take a look at our driver.'

Scott and I looked. The driver leaned over to open the passenger door, grinning at us hugely. He had abandoned his plumed hat, but still wore the extra outsize buff jerkin that I had noticed in the procession.

'We-ell, hi there, Willy!' said Scott eagerly. 'Hey, how did you come to be mixed up in all this?'

Nicolas motioned us impatiently inside. 'Here, both of you, in the back with Dr Lorenz. Sorry, it's a squeeze, Doctor. This is the young lady I was telling you about. Right, Willy, as quick as you can.'

Dr Lorenz looked alarmingly frail; his face was thin and almost as white as his hair, though he was by no means an elderly man. His physical health had obviously been affected by his incarceration, and he was worried by the motion of the car as Willy bounced it skilfully down the dirt road, into the valley and then westwards. But he was perfectly lucid. He glanced at me shyly, and thanked me for changing places with his daughter.

'How was Elisabeth when you saw her in Berlin?' he asked anxiously.

'Very well, as far as I could tell. But you'll see her for yourself when you get to West Berlin, Dr Lorenz.

We never managed to complete the second part of the exchange, you see. I'm sorry about that – I know she didn't want to leave the East. I hope she won't hate me for it.'

His gaunt face slowly relaxed into an unpractised smile. 'I think,' he said gently, 'that she will live to thank you as much as I do.'

Nicolas turned in his seat to speak to me. 'You've been lucky, you know,' he said sternly. 'Oh, I realise that things went wrong through no fault of yours, but you haven't exactly been co-operative, have you? Even if Braun hadn't been playing a double game, you could so easily have messed things up by not doing as you were told. You were mad to take that lipstick into East Berlin! And what have you been doing in the town just now? Your shopping?'

'Shopping?' I exploded.

'Shopping?' echoed Scott indignantly. 'Alison has been really great, helping you and all. Let me tell you how she got rid of that man Braun for you – if it hadn't been for her –'

He told the story, playing up my part and making light of his own, but he didn't demur when I corrected the emphasis. When he'd finished, Nicolas turned round sufficiently in his seat to look Scott firmly in the eye. 'You young idiot . . . ' he said.

I opened my mouth to protest on Scott's behalf, but saw the look they were exchanging – adult, masculine, appreciative – and knew that any intervention was unnecessary.

Nicolas's long-lashed eyes slid towards mine. 'As for you,' he said ominously, 'I'll talk to you later . . . '

*

Willy stopped the car just inside a wood on the edge of a quiet valley. The sun had gone down completely, but there was still an hour before dark. Ahead of us lay a level meadow, thick with wild flowers that had already folded their petals for the night. On the far side of the meadow, the land rose to a wooded ridge.

Nicolas motioned us quietly out of the car and towards the fringe of the wood. He and Willy had to support Dr Lorenz, who seemed very weak, and Scott hovered solicitously behind me. My arm was no longer bleeding, but it felt stiff and sore.

We all moved forward as inconspicuously as possible and crouched in a dry thistly ditch at the edge of the meadow. Willy pointed up to the crest of the ridge, less than half a mile away.

'That is where the border is,' he said. 'You see the watch tower, over the trees there? This is as close as I dare bring you.'

'Close enough,' said Nicolas. 'Listen, then, Alison. The chopper will be coming over the border to land in this meadow in about three minutes time – you made us cut it pretty fine. Once it approaches the border, the guards will know what it's up to and all hell will be let loose. They're bound to fire at it, and they'll also call up reinforcements. So the pilot has to hop in and out again as quickly as possible, and we mustn't delay him. The minute he comes in to land, we run out to him. Scott will help you aboard – right, Scott?'

'Right!' Scott lay on his stomach between us, his eyes gleaming again. I only hoped that his friends would believe all his stories when he got home.

I raised my head and looked across at Willy. 'You will make sure that Scott gets back to the camp safely, won't you, Willy?' I begged.

'Of course, of course,' Willy answered with comforting matter-of-factness.

'Stop fussing, Alison,' growled Nicolas. 'It's a bit late for you to worry about Scott's welfare – we needn't have brought him if you hadn't been shaken up and injured, and *that* would never have happened if you'd had the sense to wait by the car.'

I caressed my sore arm. 'Thank you for your gratitude,' I said.

'Oh, I'm not ungrateful – as it happened, it turned

out well. But when I think of the risk you ran . . . it was a fool thing to do, Alison! You should have left Braun to us. Willy and I are professionals, we're prepared for trouble and we know how to deal with it. Next time you're out with me, for heaven's sake do as you're told!'

I was too weary and sore to endure any more of Nicolas's arrogance. Suddenly I remembered his infuriating attitude when he had tried to kiss me beside the Havel; was he now according me the privilege of joining the ranks of his girlfriends, on condition that I did as I was told?

I nudged Scott. 'You might care to tell your friend,' I said, 'that I don't accept invitations on those terms!'

Scott was clearly divided by his admiration for Nicolas, a gallant desire to support me and a healthy respect for the rights of women. 'Er – you heard that?' he asked Nicolas diplomatically.

'Yes. But you might like to point out to your friend that as soon as we get back to England, I'm resigning from this job. As from next month, I'll be farming.'

'Really?' Scott couldn't hide his disappointment, but he turned to me seriously. 'That's a safer occupation,' he advised.

'It's his attitude that I object to,' I pointed out. 'I'm not interested in going out with men who try to insist that I should do things solely on their terms.'

Scott passed on part of the message: 'Alison says she's not interested. That's not true, of course,' he added gratuitously.

'I'm glad you think so. The point is, Scott, Alison and I have a date for the weekend – I'm taking her sailing. And as a novice in a boat, she'll have to learn to do what she's told whether she likes it or not, or we'll capsize. Unless she's prepared to give me a guarantee of co-operation, I'm not prepared to teach her to sail.'

Scott nudged me enthusiastically. 'Hey – Nic's going to teach you to sail! *That*'s all he meant!'

My arm had begun to throb. 'I don't want to learn to sail,' I said sourly.

Scott consulted Nicolas: 'Is that true?'

'No – she was very keen last time we talked about it. You might remind her, though, that we'll be living within a couple of miles of the coast. I'm certainly hoping to have a wife who shares my enthusiasm for sailing.'

Scott turned his head towards me. 'He says to tell you – ' he began, and then his face split with a huge grin. 'Hey, Alison, did you hear that? Nic just proposed!'

I sat up, the pain in my arm forgotten, and looked uncertainly at Nicolas. 'Did you?' I asked.

He too was sitting up, looking slightly surprised, a little defiant, and extraordinarily pleased with himself.

'As a matter of fact,' he said, 'I think I did . . . '

'Get down, both!' snapped Willy urgently. 'I hear the helicopter. You must not give our position before it comes.'

We all crouched. I could hear it too, like the angry buzzing of a hornet, coming nearer and nearer. There was a distant rattle of gunfire from the watch tower, the blare of a siren, and then I could see the helicopter coming in fast from behind the ridge.

Nicolas tapped Scott's shoulder. 'Thank you for looking after Alison for me. If you don't mind helping Willy with Dr Lorenz, I'll look after her from now on.'

Scott turned to me with a cheeky grin. 'So what do I tell Nic from you, now that he's proposed?'

I smiled at the boy. 'I think,' I said, 'that this is one thing that I'd rather like to tell him myself.'

The helicopter roared towards us and then hovered like a science-fiction insect fifty feet above the meadow. It began to descend, its turbulence flattening the long flowery grasses.

We all stood up and Nicolas came to me, his hands reaching out to help me, his hair blowing in the wind, his eyes never leaving mine.

And then we all ran, ducking under the turbulence.

The helicopter landed, the doors opened, arms were stretched out to help us aboard. Scott and Willy lifted up Dr Lorenz then waved, turned and ran for cover.

The engine throbbed noisily and the whole helicopter vibrated. Nicolas crouched beside me near the open door, holding me tightly as we watched the two figures disappear into the safety of the trees. And then the engine note changed as the helicopter rose high, whirling us up and over the border to freedom and on our way towards the Norfolk coast, the sailing boat, and the Georgian house with its avenue of linden trees.

You will now want to read

OVERTURE IN VENICE

also by Hester Rowan

THE DEADLY ENCOUNTER . . .

The stranger who tried to talk to Clare Lambert at a café table in St. Mark's Square was shabby, furtive and obviously frightened. He wanted to tell her something – but she, an English tourist in Venice, couldn't understand a word of his garbled Italian. Then, the following morning, the shabby man was found murdered, and Clare became involved in a bizarre and chilling mystery that was to turn her dream holiday into a nightmare. That encounter in St. Mark's Square had put her life in danger, and only one man – the handsome, sardonic Guy Lombardi – could help her. But despite the fact that she was falling in love with Guy, Clare could not bring herself to trust him. And Guy, in his turn, believed that Clare wasn't quite as innocent as she appeared . . .

You will also enjoy reading

LOVE'S PERILOUS PASSAGE

Emma Woodhouse

LOVE IN DANGER!

Queen's Pleasance, the elegant country home of the Armitages, seems like an idyll to Gillian Wheatley when she leaves London to become governess to Poppy, the family's nine-year-old daughter. She is immediately attracted to Gavin, the Armitages' arrogant but astonishingly handsome eldest son, and despite her determination to stay aloof, soon finds herself falling in love with him. But she is confused by Gavin's attitude to her, which swings unpredictably between friendliness and contempt.

Then, like a bolt from the blue, danger strikes at Queen's Pleasance – and Gillian is caught up in a perilous kidnapping plot that threatens her and her young charge. Gillian's life is at stake – and only Gavin can help her.
But will he? . . .

0 7221 9283 5 ROMANCE 75p

MORE CLASSICAL ROMANCES FROM SPHERE

CINDERELLA IN SUNLIGHT

Hermina Black

To Barbary it was like a dream come true – here she was a guest in a lovely château in the South of France with darling Ricky. But Barbary's engagement to Ricky seemed to turn his whole world against her. Even the glamour of her stay in France could not disguise the fact that most people, from Ricky's Aunt Melisande to his oldest friend, Lady Marigold, thought her a most unsuitable match for him.

A wonderful story of sunlight and romance.

0 7221 1686 1 ROMANCE 65p

IN PURSUIT OF PERILLA

Hermina Black

Perilla was as unsophisticated as she was beautiful. Some of her colleagues at the couturier's where she worked would have called her prim. In fact, she was neither prim nor cold, just wary of the casual admirers who flocked around model girls.

Secretly she had her own ideal of the kind of man who would awaken her sleeping heart. Brant Rossiter certainly didn't fit her ideals – he was out for what he could get – and this time that meant Perilla.

Luckily she had an unlikely guardian angel in the form of Luke . . .

0 7221 1689 6 ROMANCE 65p

Also available from Sphere Books

THE GIRL FROM VAN LEYDENS

Hermina Black

Prunella stared in amazement at the treasure in her hands – one of the most beautiful illuminated manuscripts in the world, a rare and lovely 'Book of Hours'. As a partner in a great antiquarian bookselling firm she was delighted at her find, and doubly so since the manuscript belonged to the man she loved – Giles – and Prunella had discovered it for him. The one fly in the ointment was Noel, Giles' handsome cousin. If Giles were to marry Prunella, Noel would lose his claim to the family fortune, so the marriage had to be stopped at all costs.

ENCHANTED OASIS

Hermina Black

An unexpected meeting with a rich American friend and her offer of a job abroad transformed Bryony's dull existence. The enchantment of Morocco was a far cry from her life of drudgery as a twentieth-century Cinderella with a demanding step-mother and step-sisters. In Casablanca, Bryony met the handsome Grant Beresford – and immediately lost her heart. Grant seemed to return her love and Bryony was ecstatic with happiness. Everything was so wonderful! Too wonderful to be true . . .

0 7221 1691 8 65p